Karma:
The Journey of a Young Poet
by Miguel Bash

KARMA: THE JOURNEY OF A YOUNG POET
BY MIGUEL BASH

Editing and Interior Layout by Urban Book Editor
Cover Design by Bowman Artistic Designs

Published by Trendstar Publishing, PO Box 555134, Orlando, FL 32855

Printed in the United States of America.

ISBN-13: 978-1-7375248-1-6
ISBN-10: 1-7375248-1-3

Library of Congress Control Number: 2021916855

10 9 8 7 6 5 4 3 2
First Edition

This novel is a work of fiction. Any references to real people, family, events, establishments, or locales are intended to give the story a sense of reality and authenticity. Other names, places, characters, brands, companies, and any incidents occurring in the works are either the product of the author's imagination or are used fictitiously.

Dedication

I dedicate this book to my son, Kefir Warrior Bashford. I remember waking up during night-time hours to complete this book because you were a toddler who kept me too busy during the day. You have reassured me that nothing is impossible.

Acknowledgments

I would like to acknoledge my mother and my siblings for inspiring and supporting me through thick and thin.

My late grandmother, Lillie Bell McDonald, for being a great role model and an example of unconditional love.

The teachers at Miami Carol City Sr. High who noticed my talent and advised me to never stop writing.

My editor and self-publishing coach, Michele Barard, for clarifying certain aspects of writing and walking me through the process of publishing books.

And, finally, the younger generations of my family who inspire me to create a legacy from which they will benefit in the future.

Table of Contents

Chapter 1

One evening, Jeffrey Jacob found himself in what looked like an abandoned village, and he was running through it with all his strength. No one was physically chasing him, but he was running away from a series of bad luck. Minutes later, he was lifted off his feet as if he were being raptured, and then, he landed in a populated city. The city was filled with high-rise buildings, lights, glamour, and friendly people. He noticed that almost everyone was heading in the same direction, to an open park down the street, where thousands of people were gathered. As he approached, the noise from the crowd grew louder and louder, and when he made it to the stage area, he noticed that a door was left open. He was curious, and so he went inside to see what was going on. To his surprise, he had just walked through the entrance to the backstage of an ongoing concert. He peeked through the curtains at the audience and saw thousands of excited people full of energy. He also noticed that the microphone was standing alone on stage. He realized that everyone was awaiting the next performer. At that moment, he felt relieved from the pressure that he was dealing with. Without second-guessing, he walked across the stage's platform towards the microphone. It was intensive, as the audience clapped and cheered him on…

"Wake up, Son," said Ms. Elaine as she shook the sleeping lad. "It is almost dinner time, and the guests will be arriving soon."

He was shocked when he opened his eyes and checked his surroundings; it was unbelievable that what felt so tangible was only a dream.

"Ok, Ma," Jeffrey mumbled. He had been up early that morning, helping his mother in the kitchen, and then after that, he took an afternoon nap.

It was Thanksgiving Day of 2001, and their two-story house outside of the Magnolia complex in New Orleans was filled with the aromas of delicious foods. Jeffrey, who was 12 years old, lived with his mother, Elaine Johnson, who most people called Ms. Elaine or Ms. Johnson because she was a teacher. His family was well known in the neighborhood, primarily because of his father, Jimmy Jacob, who had his own house Uptown. Jimmy and Elaine lived separately because of their different lifestyles, but they were still undeniably in love. They kept close contact so that Jimmy could be in his son's life as much as possible, and one thing for sure, the family was well taken care of.

"Jeff, are you feeling ok?" His mother asked.

"Yes, mom, I was dreaming," Jeffrey replied as he sat up. "I was in front of thousands of people, and I was just about to entertain them with some lyrics."

"Is that right?" Ms. Elaine laughed. "Ok, Mr. Microphone checker! I'm sorry if I interrupted."

"It's ok, Ma," said Jeffrey, as he stood up and stretched, and then he hugged his mother and kissed her. "I love you, Mommy."

"Ah, you are so sweet! I love you more, my son, and I pray that one day, all your dreams do come true," she replied as they hugged each other.

"Thank you, mother. I know they will," said Jeffrey, and then he began to sniff the air. "It sure does smell good up in here, though!"

Ms. Elaine smiled, and then she said: "This is a day of thanksgiving, gratitude, and a lot of food. So, freshen up and get dressed. Your aunty Suzan and your dad are on their way over." Suzan is Elaine's sister, and Michael is her 4-year-old son.

"Yes! Daddy's coming," said Jeffrey excitingly. "And I get to see my little cousin, Michael!"

"That's right! So, chop-chop," Ms. Elaine replied and smiled as she walked off.

"I'll be downstairs in no time, Mama!" Jeffrey yelled as he hurried to the bathroom for a shower.

New Orleans was full of excitement; almost every day, there was a party, a festival, or some type of celebration. Mardi Gras, Thanksgiving, Christmas, and birthdays were always worth looking forward to. However, there were also many gangs and turf wars, and those rivalries resulted in many murders. The crime stemmed from various low-income neighborhoods or the projects. Nevertheless, grown folk's business did not stop Jeffrey from enjoying his childhood. The same attitude was shared amongst his peers; they were growing up in a world of their own. Jeff, a.k.a. Little Jeff, or Lil Jeff, was popular. He was always clean and fresh, and his style was neat and unique. With his parents' support, especially his dad, anything he wanted was regularly available to him.

Moreover, he was an A student because solutions to problems came to him quickly if he was focused. There was no reason for him not to focus; therefore, he was always on the honor roll. His mother was a high school English teacher, and with her guidance, he grew to love reading books and even writing some of his own works. His hobbies were, playing basketball with his friends and reciting his poems. Growing up, Jeffrey had everything that a kid could ever want, from the latest gadgets to the newest Air Jordans. He never really knew what his father did for a living, and he never really cared to ask. However, Jimmy was a career criminal who was on top of his game. He and Elaine were high school sweethearts. Elaine was that beautiful girl who was always focused on her studies, the type of girl who made a guy check himself before he approached her.

On the other hand, Jimmy was a charmer who would put his all into getting anything he really wanted. He was street-smart and knew how to carry himself. Furthermore, Elaine was the girl he wanted to be with, and he did not stop trying to impress her until she fell in love with him. Their first date was the senior prom. After that, there was no looking back. The love birds hit it off, and about a year after high school, they shared their first apartment together; they were two great minds, planning to start a family and build an empire. It was around that time that baby Jeffrey, their only child, was conceived. Unfortunately, after a few years of living together, Jimmy and Elaine slowly drifted apart. Jimmy could not leave the streets alone. Even though he was still in love with Elaine, he was at his pivot, and he wanted to keep the money flowing. Therefore, he decided to live elsewhere to protect his woman and their son. Jimmy was the financial anchor of the family. He took care of all the expenses and visited them as often as his time allowed.

Jeffery showered quickly and got dressed, and then he went straight downstairs to join the feast. His aunt and his cousin were already there, and he hugged and kissed his aunty, and then he picked up little Michael. After a while, he stepped into the kitchen, and he saw containers of all sizes filled with different foods. His mother loved to cook, and every year, Thanksgiving was one of the most highly anticipated holidays. This time, the menu consisted of roast turkey, grilled fish, fried chicken, barbecue chicken, sausage gumbo, mac -n- cheese, rice -n- peas, collard greens, potato salad, cornbread, banana pudding, and Jeffrey's favorite, sweet potato pie.

"You came just in time to set the table," said Ms. Elaine to Jeffrey.

"The pleasure is all mines," he replied as he fetched plates and utensils. He set up the table with glasses, plates, knives, forks, and the food in the middle.

The doorbell rang just as everyone was about to sit down. "I got it," said Jeffrey as he ran to the door. It was exactly who he was expecting. "Daddy!" he yelled and threw his arms around his father.

"What's up, my boy!" Jimmy replied. "How you been?"

"I been great, dad!" said Jeffrey. "I just finished setting the table. You are right on time."

"That's wonderful," said Jimmy, then he turned around and called his partner, who was still in the car. "Hey Boe, come on in, Bro!" Boe was his right-hand man, who was well familiar with the family.

"Is that Jim?" Elaine asked as she came to the doorway.

"Yes, sweetheart, it's me," Jimmy replied as he passed his son and walked up to his lady to hug her. They still shared that sparkle in their eyes whenever they saw each other.

"Waddup, Lil Jeff?" said Boe, who walked up to the door, giving the youngster a handshake as he entered the house.

"What's up, OG!" Jeffrey replied, and he closed the door behind them.

"Elaine, how you doing? It smells like you put your foot in this one!" said Boe, and everyone laughed.

"Hey, how are you, Mr. Boe?" she replied. "We were just about to eat. I hope you guys are hungry."

Jimmy and Boe replied simultaneously. "Starving!"

Ms. Elaine smiled. "Well then, let us meet at the dinner table."

After the fellows greeted Suzan and Michael, everyone sat at the dinner table, intending to satisfy their taste buds.

"Wait a minute now," said Suzan. "First, let us pray." They all agreed, and then they joined hands and closed their eyes. Suzan began. "God is good, God is great. We thank You, Father, for this food and for this family. Please allow us to see many more times like this. Amen!"

"Amen!" said everyone together, and then the feast began.

Jeffrey would often hear rumors about his father's actions in the streets. Even though his family was well respected, he knew some people could not be trusted. Jimmy never explained the details of his business. Still, around town, he was known as a sharpshooter, a terror to his rivals. He made his money the fast way but avoided anything petty; he only went on big heists and contract assassinations. People called him "One-Shot" because that was all he needed to cancel his opponent many times. Jimmy "One-Shot" Jacob was his name, and it rang bells in the city; he was a 3rd Ward official gangster. New Orleans was like the Wild Wild West in the late nineties and early two-thousands. The murder rate was steadily increasing, and drugs and guns were spreading like wildfire. One-Shot and his partners formed an alliance called the Notorious Triple Beam Gang, the TBG for short. The three main leaders were Jimmy, OG Boe, and Ramon Dollars; they had the money, power, and respect they demanded. Their most formidable rivals were from the Calliope project, who always went back and forth with them, murder after murder. However, the TBG also extended fear throughout different neighborhoods around New Orleans. They were known for pulling off some of the biggest robberies.

Nevertheless, Jimmy was a one-man army, and he handled most of his endeavors by himself. When a job was too big for him to handle alone, he would team up with Boe and Ramon. Ramon was a big-time drug dealer; he had one of the best suppliers that an average hustler could come across, and the dope fiends were ready to sell their souls just for a taste of the rock. Boe, a tall dude with a peanut-shaped head, kept the project in check, controlling the circulation of the guns and the ammunition. He was a 3rd Ward OG and the TBG's getaway driver.

The family laughed and talked as they enjoyed Ms. Elaine's top-class cooking, and over an hour passed before anyone moved. Then, Jimmy excused himself from the table to smoke a cigarette out front, and Jeffrey got up and followed him. OG Boe was still munching, and so was Elaine and her sister; everyone ate at least two or three plates, and there was still plenty of food left.

When they made it outside, Jimmy lit a Newport and then began talking to Jeffrey. "Hey, son, seems like you're getting bigger every time I see you. So, is there anything you want to tell me?"

"Not really, Daddy. Only that I am glad to see you," Jeffrey replied.

There was much compassion in Jimmy's eyes. As rough as he was in the streets, he was soft-hearted when it came to his family. "I want you to have something," he said and then reached into his pocket and pulled out a gold ring with a diamond pyramid on top. "This is the first pinky ring I ever bought. It represents strength and unity, and it's very special. I want you to have it."

Little Jeff was flattered. It meant the world to him; he put the ring on his right-hand middle finger, which was a perfect fit.

"Thank you, Dad. I love it," said Jeffrey.

"You are welcome, my son. Try not to lose it," Jimmy replied.

Then, he reached into his pocket again, and this time, he gave Jeffrey a thousand dollars and told him to save it. Then, he gave him five more crispy hundred-dollar bills and said, "That's for your pockets."

"Ok, Daddy. Thank you! I love you," said Jeffrey.

"I love you too, Jeff. Just keep on being brilliant and making us proud," Jimmy replied, and they hugged.

Minutes later, OG Boe came out, looking as stuffed like a teddy bear. "Boss man, we still on schedule?" he asked.

"Oh yeah, most definitely. Give me a minute, let me wrap it up with the fam," said Jimmy, and then he went back inside the house to touch base with Elaine.

"Hey, honey, you did it again! Everything was wonderful. Thank you so much, my love," said Jimmy. "I have to make a run now, but hold on to this," he continued as he handed her an envelope.

The envelope had ten thousand dollars in it, and Ms. Elaine, who was used to him coming through in that type of way, was profoundly grateful. "Ok, Jim, thank you! And please be careful out there," she replied while looking into his eyes. Then, she gave him a bag with to-go plates that she fixed for Boe and him.

"No, my love, thank you. You are the best," said Jimmy, as he gave her a tight hug and a kiss. Afterward, he went back out front.

Little Jeff was out there entertaining Boe with some of his rhymes when Jimmy walked out. Jimmy laughed, and then he hugged his son and said, "See you later, big man."

"Later, dad, and later OG!" Jeffrey replied. Then, Jimmy and Boe got into the black Mercedes Benz parked on the curb and drove off.

Chapter 2

The TBG planned to rob a Brinks truck, a job worth a couple hundred thousand dollars or more. The crew had been watching the truck for over two weeks, learning the route and the pickup locations, switching up vehicles to remain unnoticed. The day of the operation came, they followed the truck to its last pickup stop, a Walgreens. After timing the guard who walked out with the money bag, Jimmy and Ramon ran down on him with their handguns without hesitating. The security guard saw them approaching with ski masks on and tried to reach for his pistol; Jimmy shot him one time in his head, and he fell backward. Then, Ramon ran up and grabbed the money bag while Jimmy covered him. As they tried to run back to the getaway vehicle, the driver of the Brinks truck started shooting with an automatic rifle. Jimmy and Ramon were running and dodging at the same time.

OG Boe saw the action and got ready, placing the transmission in drive as his partners jumped into the vehicle. Then, he stepped on the gas in a hurry, and they were off with the cash. However, they had opened a can of worms. Every police unit that was in the area was now on their trail. The robbery developed into a high-speed chase. Boe gave it all he had, bending corners until they made it onto the interstate, where he switched lanes at a rapid pace. He was doing the whole dash for over an hour of reckless driving and interstate rivalry. However, the police stayed on them until they managed to shoot out the tires, causing Boe to spin out of control. He crashed into another vehicle so hard that the getaway car flipped over and landed upside down. The sight was breathtaking, and everyone thought that they were all dead. In the front passenger seat, Ramon was bleeding from his head, and he was not moving. Jimmy and Boe happened to crawl from under the vehicle, bruised and in pain. When they looked up, they saw that they were surrounded by policemen, who had their guns drawn. Boe did the best thing at that point: to lay flat on the ground with his hands in sight, but Jimmy did the opposite. He made a terrible decision to open fire. Therefore, the cops returned fire, and they got the best of him, killing him execution-style.

Three years after Jimmy died, Ms. Elaine packed up all her belongings, and she and Jeffrey migrated to Miami. She wanted a fresh start, and after visiting Miami, a couple times with Jimmy, she decided that it was the closest place to her hometown. It was becoming difficult for her to maintain the lifestyle that they lived when Jimmy was alive. Because he took care of so many expenses, everything had been much more manageable. Besides, there had been a sudden buildup of backlash and criticism from different people around town, and they did not know who to trust. Therefore, she gathered up all the money she had put away and used it as a down payment on a three-bedroom house in Miami Gardens, Florida. She wanted to get away from everything and everyone back home and start a new life with her son in The Sunshine State.

They went through the hassle of the moving process, and they were now settling in and getting used to the environment of south Florida. Even though it had been two years since they were there, they have not done much socializing with anyone in the neighborhood, only in school, where Jeffrey did meet a few friends. For Ms. Elaine, it was all work and no play; she found a job as a teacher at Miami Carol City Sr. High school, the same school that Jeffrey was attending. He was a junior, and he was doing well in his classes. Ms. Elaine was a 9th grade English teacher, and she volunteered to do after-school tutoring to pick up some overtime.

Jeffrey had recently celebrated his 17th birthday with his mother. The summer break was drawing near, and everyone seemed to be in their own world of ideas. There was also always something disturbing on the news. Street life in Miami was transitioning from the cocaine era, which had produced many cold-blooded murderers, ruthless gangs, and organized crimes. From the 1980s up to the late-'90s, the violence in Miami was at an all-time high, with dominance from street gangs like John Doe, Zoe Pound, and the Boobie Boys, just to name a few. They all existed in the same city, around the same time, causing the streets to be on fire literally. However, with due diligence from law enforcement, the best tactics were used to intercept operations and illustrate law and order. The police force raided many dope-holes and demolished a few apartment complexes where the violence was heavy. The kingpins from that era either died in a gun battle or are still in prison today. However, their protégés were now on the rise, and they all had a point to prove. The younger generations ushered the new era, trying to make a name for themselves in the streets. They amplified themselves with drugs from cocaine to ecstasy pills, and then robbing and killing became a sport. There wasn't half as much cocaine as there was in the '80s, but guns and ammunition never seized to flow.

Jeffrey and his mother went to school together in the mornings. In the afternoon, he left school at 2:30 p.m. when class was over and worked on homework while waiting for his mom to get home. Ms. Elaine did after-school tutoring from 3 to 6 p.m. They lived about 30 minutes from the school, and one bus took them back and forth. Ms. Elaine usually made it home around 6:45 p.m., just in time to catch the 7 o'clock news. However, this day was unusual. It was already 6:55, and for some reason, she was nowhere in sight. Jeffrey tried to stay positive, but he started to worry a little, and he constantly peeked out the window. For dinner, they were going to eat leftovers from the night before. He had already taken the food from the refrigerator and placed the pots on the stove under low heat, just like she had told him. By ten minutes after seven, he knew that something was wrong. His instincts led him to turn the TV to the local news channel. There was a breaking news story, and the reporter was live at the scene.

"We are here live on the corner of 199th street and 37th avenue, where less than an hour ago, a woman was robbed and gunned down. Witnesses say that she may have been coming home from work...," the reporter went on, and her words echoed in Jeffrey's head.

He froze, and the remote fell from his hand, his countenance saddened, and he staggered. When his brain re-activated, he stormed through the front door and ran full speed to the scene of the crime. As he got closer to 37th avenue, he heard the sirens, making his heartbeat speed up. Then, when he came in clear view of the yellow tapes, tears began to flow from his eyes; yet he was still hoping that it was not her. He arrived at the crime scene heavily breathing and pushing his way through the crowd of people gathered to look. Jeffrey tried his best to get a glimpse as the body was being carried to the ambulance.

"Let me through," he cried.

Then, he ducked under the tapes and ran towards the paramedics, who were almost at the ambulance. He recognized the clothes and realized that it was his mother. He was devasted, and immediately, he blacked out and collapsed. The silence of his mind overpowered the chaotic scenery until he felt the grip of a police officer who was pulling him by the arm.

"Boy, what's the matter with you? No one is allowed under the tapes!" The officer yelled, but Jeffrey laid there looking clueless.

"Please! Everyone, stand back," said another policeman to the people who were gliding closer and closer to the tapes to get a better view. Their voices filled the air as they made comments and asked random questions.

"Is she still breathing?" A woman asked.

Eventually, Jeffrey opened his eyes and woke up to what he wished was a dream. When he realized that it was real, he began to plead. "That's my mother! They shot my mom!" Jeffrey cried, stuttering with bitterness, as the pain ran deep inside his body.

"Say what? Hey, Sarg! This young man is saying that the victim is his mother," said the officer who held him to a man who was wearing a blue suit.

"Let him up, Tony! Let him up," the man in the suit replied.

Jeffrey swiveled away from Tony's restraint and made his way to the ambulance where his mother was. When he climbed into the truck, the paramedics were administering CPR. She was barely breathing. He cried and waited until they completed the procedure, and then he went up to her and hugged her closely. At that moment, everything quelled.

"Hey, Mom, it's me, Jeff. Please, Mama, don't go," he begged as he held her.

She had been shot twice, in her stomach and chest, and the wounds were still visible; it was a bloody sight indeed. Jeffrey continued to hold her, and her blood was now all over him. Then suddenly, Ms. Elaine, who had only a slight pulse, felt the presence of her son, and she lifted her eyelids slightly to look.

Jeffrey's adrenaline rushed when he noticed, and he cried. "Mama, tell me who did this to you!"

Ms. Elaine whispered. "Son, just let it go." Then, she began to cough, and her eyes slowly closed. She was trying to hang in there, but the pain was unbearable; therefore, unable to prolong the suffering, she died right there in his arms. After that, the chaos resumed.

A loud beeping sound came from a machine in the ambulance, and one of the paramedics yelled. "We must leave now to the emergency room! You are welcome to come along with us," he told Jeffrey.

However, he knew that she was gone and did not want to deal with anyone questioning him because he felt mentally unbalanced. Therefore, he ignored the man's offer and jumped out of the truck without replying. They closed the doors behind him and drove off in a hurry while he stood there covered in blood. His world was crumbling, and it felt like hell on earth; he then fell to his knees, screaming and crying at the top of his lungs. It was more than a murder scene. It was mayhem as the sirens from squad cars and the ambulance collaborated.

"Oh my God! That's her son," said someone from the crowd.

Then, when Jeffrey got up from his knees, he saw the X's on the pavement, signifying the spot where she fell. He also saw the Channel 7 news crew and the same lady he had seen on TV at home doing the live report. Witnesses said they saw an unidentified black male running after the gunshots were heard, and apparently, he escaped. The cops had no leads on the suspect, but they claimed they were on top of it. The news crew approached Jeffrey for questioning, but he rejected and walked away. Overwhelmed with heartbreak and misfortune, he had no energy for a conversation of any sort; the only thing he felt was a strong urge for revenge. Besides, he was not familiar with any of the present faces. Therefore, he just ran back towards the house. His mother's death was a hard pill to swallow. As the sound of the sirens became distant, so did the love in his heart. That night, Jeffrey was unable to sleep, dwelling on the fact that she was really gone.

Chapter 3

A few days later, one early morning, Jeffrey was at home in the bathroom mirror, reciting one of his favorite poems, and he began:

"So, I write!
When I was born, there was no material wealth
for me to inherit. But I grew to realize
that the creativity of my mindset
holds more value than diamonds.
Indeed, I am one of the elements
when I'm in tune with nature.
Sights worth seeing are the regions
where the earth meets with existence.
And even though I tried numerous occupations
I'll never neglect
the fact of my soul's essence
which is, to Live and Serve, and to Speak
So, I write!
To reclaim the royalties of my ancestors
and to not let Mr. Garvey down.
His-tory tells his story
the blood runs through my veins.
I refuse to be another victim
destroyed by the hands of poverty.
So, to free my mind
I write!

When the fighter wants to keep on fighting,
but the coach says it's over.
I write when my deepest emotions
cannot be expressed as tears or laughter.
After everything that we been through!
Oh, I gotta make it count.
So, I write!"

The days that followed the incident were miserable, and Jeffrey was getting little to no sleep. On and on, the tragedy continued to plague his mind; he was not sure which direction to turn for help, so he cried until his tears ran dry. Undeniably, his mother was all he had, and he was afraid to face the reality of not having her around. Moreover, he wanted to find the man who pulled the trigger and look him in the eyes before killing him. The first time his mother told him about the idea of moving to Miami, he did not like it because he did not want to leave the friends that he had grown up with. However, she was sick and tired of the criticism and the threats that followed them after Jimmy died. Some people were even claiming that he owed them money. Therefore, she had her mind set on moving, and Little Jeff was left without a choice, so in December of 2004, they moved to South Florida. Coincidentally, they were fortunate enough to escape a disaster because Hurricane Katrina destroyed parts of New Orleans just months after they left. Almost a year after Katrina, they were still unable to locate or contact anyone they knew. Their family was among the many that were missing. Last Christmas break, Ms. Elaine took a trip back home by herself to search for her parents and sister; however, she was unsuccessful in finding them. The area where they lived had been destroyed, and the city looked completely different. She had planned to visit again during the upcoming summer break, and this time Jeffrey was supposed to accompany her. It would be his first time going back since they left, and he was really looking forward to it. Unfortunately, his mother's death changed everything, and now he had to figure life out on his own.

During his misery, he asked the universe: "What is life to be desired if such a bond be broken?"

Ms. Elaine's funeral only housed a few people, most of whom were members of the church. Nevertheless, the ceremony was warm and touching, and Jeffrey was there, still wishing that it was all just a bad dream that he would soon wake up from. After his mother's burial, his future stood undoubtedly uncertain. Jeffrey tried to be tough. He knew that is what she would have wanted. He had found some money that his mother was saving, and it was enough for him to pay a couple of months forward on the mortgage and buy groceries. He even tried to go back to school and finish up because he only had one year left to graduate after all. Unfortunately, he could not focus, especially since some of the students knew about the tragedy, and they kept asking him questions. He never did express to anyone how he felt because he did not want to host a pity party. So, eventually, he stopped going to school altogether. Before his mother's death, Jefferey was doing exceptionally well in school; just like that, his reality changed, and it was now time to face the unexpected. Everything that he needed was inside the house. So, to maintain his sanity, he avoided people by staying in there. However, before he knew it, three months had passed, and he knew that he had to pull it together and get out into the world. There were bills to pay, and he had to put food on the table.

When he finally went outside, the first thing he did was check the mailbox. He found nothing but past due bills, an electric bill, a cable bill, and a letter from the mortgage lender about not receiving payment for the previous month. The letter also noted that he had 30 days to clear the balance, or else there would be an eviction. Little Jeff was overwhelmed, but he wanted to maintain the expenses and keep the house. His mother was never late with her bills, and she always taught him to be responsible. He figured that the best thing to do was get a job and start making money right away.

The next day Jeffrey dressed neatly and went out early to look for work. He started at the new shopping plaza on 199th street and 27th avenue, and then he worked his way north towards Miramar Parkway.

In the shopping plaza on Miramar Parkway and 27th Avenue, he came upon a small grocery store called SAM'S, and he went in there to see if they were hiring. It was a Caribbean convenient store with a restaurant in the back. Jeffrey spoke to an elderly man at the register, who introduced himself as Sam.

"Good morning! Are you guys hiring?" Jeffrey asked.

"As a matter of fact, we are," Sam replied. "We could use someone to stack the shelves and clean up. You will make $250 a week."

"Yeah, I can do that," said Jeffrey without second-guessing.

"Well, if you want the job, be here tomorrow at 8 a.m.," Sam replied.

"You got it, sir! See you tomorrow morning," said Jeffrey. It was his first real job, and he was excited. The following day, he sat at the bus stop, waiting for the northbound 27A bus. He had been out there since 7 a.m., dressed in a sweater and jeans because it was a windy morning. The time on his watch read 7:30, and there was still no bus in sight; he was starting to worry that he would be late on his first day at work. He was nervous and checked his watch frequently; the bus was usually on time, rarely, like that day morning it would be held up for some reason. The time read 7:43 when he finally saw it coming, and he got up quickly to wave it down. The bus driver pulled up slowly to the bus stop and opened the doors, and then Jeffrey got in and paid his bus fare. The ride to SAM'S took about 20 minutes, including stops to pick up and drop off passengers. Still, Jeffrey was trying to keep hope alive. The last thing that he wanted to hear was that he lost the job before he even started, especially when he was really trying to do the right thing. Furthermore, when he got off the bus at Miramar Parkway, it was 10 minutes after 8. He power-walked past the Shell gas station, then past the Presidente grocery store, where SAM'S was located around the corner.

"I thought I said 8 a.m.!" said the boss sarcastically when Jeffrey walked into the store.

"Yes, sir, you did, but the bus had a delay," he replied.

"Well, that is not my problem. I'm going to let you pass today, but if you want to keep this job, you need to be here on time," said Sam. He was a short, light-skinned man in his early fifties, somewhat arrogant, with an untouchable attitude.

"No problem, sir," Jeffrey replied. He was glad that he was not fired.

Sam pointed towards the kitchen area. "Head to the back. Your co-worker, Kevin, will show you what to do."

"Yes, sir," said Jeffrey. "Oh, good morning, by the way," he added as he walked off.

The boss stared at him without responding, and Jeffrey made his way to the back of the store to meet Kevin. When he went through the transparent blinds, he saw a shabby-looking guy in the small kitchen, prepping the food for the day. "Are you Kevin?" he asked.

"Yah, mon, ah me that," said the guy as he looked up and smiled. One of his front teeth was missing, and the one beside it was chipped off. "Me soon come show yuh the ropes."

Jeffrey nodded, he thought it was a weird accent, but Kevin seemed like a cool guy. They had a short conversation while Jeffrey waited for him. He said that he used to stack the shelves and clean up before becoming the cook. Not long after, he paused what he was doing to show Jeffrey around the store and to lay out his job assignment. Jeffrey was to keep the shelves stacked and keep track of the inventory, letting Sam know when an item runs low. Also, he had to clean up throughout the day, sweep and mop the floor, and take the trash out before leaving at 5:30 p.m. Kevin showed him where everything was kept and where the garbage disposal was located behind the building. Then, he made his way back to the kitchen to finish what he was doing.

Jeffrey thought the job seemed like something that he could handle, and he would work there for a while to see how things played out. He was desperate for the money to catch up on the bills. He tried to make a good impression on his first day at work, starting off by restacking some shelves that he noticed were low on items. As the day went along, he learned there was a lot of work associated with the tasks of his job assignment. And he was already seeing what he was going to dislike the most, which was restacking the juices because it was super cold inside the cooler. He also noticed that Sam was even more arrogant when his buddies came in. Just for attention, one of them would complain about something in the store, which would result in Sam nagging Jeffrey to fix it. Nevertheless, staying busy consumed the time, and before you knew it, it was already 4:30. Jeffrey was stacking a row of cereals when Sam's voice broke his concentration.

"Young man, why is the floor not swept yet?" he asked.

"Oh, I'm about to get to that right after I finish this, sir," Jeffrey replied.

"Well, time is moving. Let's get to it!" Sam yelled.

"Yes, boss," said Jeffrey. Then he swept and mopped the floor and took the thrash outside.

Finally, it was 5:30, and Jeff was not going to stay a minute later; his work for the day was finished, and so he said goodbyes to everyone, and then he left. A bus pulled up to the bus stop as he approached, so he ran to it and got on it, paid his fare, and then found a seat in the back where he usually sat. When he got off the bus up the block from his house, it was a couple of minutes after 6 p.m., and he felt tired. As he walked, he thought to himself how he had just experienced a little of what his mother went through to care for them. His weariness caused him to amble while his day replayed in his head. The job was not too bad, except for the nagging boss. He decided to keep going there, hoping that his paychecks would clear up the bills and smooth things out. Fortunately, he and Kevin got along well, and he learned that the guy was a great cook. Earlier that day, he made brown stew chicken with rice-n-peas, steamed cabbage, and fried plantains. Jeffrey ate some on his 30-minute lunch break and enjoyed every bit of it. It was by far the best meal he had eaten since his mother died. When Jeffrey made it home, he took a warm shower, ate a peanut butter and jelly sandwich, and then went straight to bed. He was exhausted and wanted to rest so he could get up and do it again the next day. That night Little Jeff slept like a baby.

Chapter 4

A month later, one Friday afternoon, he was at work finishing up his shift, and he was in a good mood because it was payday. The store was filled with customers, and it had been a busy day since that morning. Jeffrey was getting through his day the same way that he did for the past month, by ignoring the boss's antics and focusing on the task at hand. He was adapting to adulthood, and he became faithful to his work schedule; he even figured out how to make it there 30 minutes early every morning. It was drawing near to 5:30 p.m., and he was outside discarding the trash. He had been on his feet all day, and now he was tired and ready to leave. He planned to wake up the following day for a bus tour of the city. Then, he would get off and check out wherever looked interesting. He and his mother were supposed to tour their new city, but time never permitted. He still wanted to see the city up close. When he went back into the store, he went to the bathroom, washed his hands, and headed to Sam's office. His purpose was to collect his fourth paycheck since he had been working. When he got to the office, he knocked twice on the door, and then, without waiting for an answer, he went in. When he entered, Sam was sitting behind his desk fumbling through some paperwork, and then he looked up with a bizarre gaze.

"All done, sir!" Jeffrey gladly interrupted.

"Alright, here you go," said Sam and handed him an envelope with $250 cash.

"Thank you, sir. See you next week," Jeffrey replied.

Sam nodded, then he ducked his head back into the paperwork, and Jeffrey turned around and walked out. He saw Kevin in the kitchen cleaning up when he was heading out, and he stopped to tell him goodbye.

"Kevin, have a good weekend!" Jeffrey shouted, to be heard above the running fossil in the sink.

"Yah, mon! Likkle more," Kevin replied, smiling and nodding at the same time.

Then, Jeffrey walked out of SAM'S and headed to the bus stop to get on the next thing smoking. He felt a big relief every time he left work and was glad to have the weekends off. That is when he felt like himself again. For the last month, his life had been a complete routine; it was a repeat of waking up and going to work, then leaving work and heading back home, just to go to sleep and wake up to do it again. He realized that such a schedule was unhealthy for him mentally, which is why he decided to ride out and clear his mind that weekend. He wanted to escape the rigid routine he viewed as a trap and see what else the city had to offer. He had used the little money he had left from his mother's savings throughout the month to pay his bus fare and buy food; and, he had saved all the money that he made at SAM'S, which was now $1,000. However, that was not enough to cover all the bills he owed because another month had accumulated. Still, he was trying to not stress himself about it. He hated the 360 turn that his life made, causing him to pay the price of responsibilities. Still, it made him mature faster, and he looked past his emotions and rose to the occasion.

When he made it to his bus stop and got off the bus, a police car drove past him, heading down his block, which made him put a pep in his step. They did not patrol the neighborhood that late unless there was an emergency or they received a call about something specific. Since Ms. Elaine died, Jeffrey was paranoid and nervous whenever he saw police cars or ambulances anywhere close to him. Therefore, he began to speed walk, and when he came into view of his house, he noticed a pile of objects on the lawn. He also saw that the squad car was pulling into his driveway, and he almost had a nervous breakdown. There was also a pick-up truck in his driveway, along with two men moving around in the yard.

"What now?" he yelled as he started running towards his house, passing a few neighbors who usually came outside to get their nose in whatever was happening.

As he got closer, it was clear to see that the objects on the lawn were furniture. He also noticed that his front door was wide open. The men were moving everything out: Tables and couches, TVs and dressers, mattresses, bed frames and carpets, all his mother's belongings were out there in the open. This was the last thing he expected after a long day of work, and he was unsure if he had the energy to deal with it.

Two officers were in the police car that pulled up, and they were just getting out when Jeffrey made it to the house; so, he went up to one of them. "Hey, can someone please tell me what the hell is going on right now?" he asked disturbingly.

The officer quickly placed his hand on his pistol in a combating gesture, and then he replied. "Sir, you need to calm down! Now, do you live here?"

Jeffrey took a deep breath. "Yes, I do! And why are these men troubling my belongings?" he asked as he took a step backward and pointed at the pile of furniture on the grass.

"Well, sir, we have an Eviction Notice, saying that you are being evicted due to consecutive months of an unpaid mortgage. Our duty here is to simply maintain the peace, so if you have a truck, you can get your belongings, but for now, the men have no choice but to leave them on the lawn."

"Eviction? Truck? No, I do not have a truck!" Jeffrey yelled. He was heated and stared at the officers puzzled; this was all new to him, and he had no idea how to navigate it. "Look, man," he continued, "I'm sure there are other ways to settle this. I have the money, ok. I'll pay what I owe first thing in the morning."

Both officers chuckled, and then the other one replied with amusement in his voice. "I'm afraid it's too late for that, son. You have reached the deadline."

"Man, come on! Please don't do this right now," Jeffrey pleaded.

However, the policeman continued to unfold the bad news. "We will allow you to run in there right now and grab any personal thing that you may need, but unfortunately, we cannot let you stay here tonight."

Jeffrey kissed his teeth and shook his head, but he kept his cool and ran in there, extremely embarrassed as he ran past the men who continued to tamper with his mother's belongings. When he went inside the house, he saw that it was nearly empty, only some small things were left. However, he went straight into his room and went to the spot where he kept his savings, and he took everything there. He also grabbed a backpack and quickly stuffed it with some hygiene products, a few T-shirts, a couple pairs of jeans, and his journal. Before he walked out the front door, he noticed a picture in a small frame on the ground and picked it up. It was an old picture of his mother and father holding him when he was only 2 years old; it was rare, so he carried it with him.

"This shit is ridiculous!" he yelled when he made it back outside.

"Hey man, we're just doing our job," one of the officers replied.

"Ok, and what the hell should I do?" Jeffrey asked angrily. His temper was boiling.

"Well, we do have some papers here for you to sign," said the policeman.

"You must be nuts! Man, I'm not signing anything."

"Ok, smart ass! Tell you what, have this junk removed from the lawn by tomorrow afternoon, or else the dump truck will swing through and get it for you. Is that clear?"

In his mind's eyes, Jeffrey saw himself telling the cops to fuck off and then grabbing one of their pistols and killing everything out there. Nothing else would satisfy him more. However, he knew that the odds were against him, so he swallowed his pride, shook his head, and just walked away without responding. It was a little after 7 p.m. and getting dark; he wandered through the neighborhood and then remembered there was a little rundown motel about three blocks up the street. He decided to crash there for the night. He was truly overwhelmed, and it was too much to process for one day. So, when he got to the motel, he paid the receptionist $80 for a room. After entering the room, he fell face-first on the bed.

The following day, he woke up early with a million things on his mind. He left the room and got on a 27A bus heading southbound. Consciously, he couldn't put a single thought together because many different scenarios were flashing through his head at a rapid pace causing him to develop a migraine. He felt terrible about the eviction, dreading the fact that he was losing everything that his mother had worked so hard for. He was beating himself up about the situation, subconsciously, wishing that he could have done more to prevent it. The summer of 2006, which was well-planned and long-awaited, got off to a bad start, to say the least. Jeffrey had no idea what to do next, and he sat there devastated, without a destination or a plan, as the bus tagged along. He was only sure about his desire to run into the fool who killed his mother. Since the cops still had no luck finding the suspect, he knew that he had to handle it himself. As far as Jeffrey was concerned, that man was responsible for the downhill turn of his life, from the tragedy to the chain reaction that followed. Everything was good before that man killed his mother. These thoughts made Jeffrey hungry for revenge. The many phases of his struggle were flashing through his mind along with childhood memories. He reflected on the murder scene and the eviction and wondered what the future would bring. The images were jumping around in his head. Then a sharp pain raced across his brain, and he dropped his head into his hands. The bus was quiet until a man sitting close to the front stood up wearing a thin blue sweater with black sweatpants began to address the passengers.

"Good morning, my brothers and sisters," said the man to

everyone on the bus.

"Good morning," said most of the passengers.

Then, the man continued. "I am compelled to share this message of encouragement with you, in the name of our Lord and Savior, Jesus Christ."

"Preach it, brother," a woman yelled.

Jeffrey lifted his head to see what was happening, and then he glanced at the time on his watch, which read 7:35 a.m. He did not care to hear the man preach, so he looked out the window, where he saw the sun brightening up the day.

However, the man went on. "I know that we all have some issues that we're facing in our lives, but I'm here this morning to tell you that it will be alright. Stay strong and keep on pushing! The race is not for the swift, but for those who can endure to the end, and god almighty will not give a man more than he can bear."

A few of the passengers shouted. "Amen to that, Brother!"

Little Jeff tried to ignore them, but it was as if the man was speaking directly to him, with a message he needed to hear. However, with the uproar in his head, the last thing he needed was more noise; so, he paid little attention and continued to fight his inner battle. At that point, the only gospel that he understood was an eye for an eye and that nothing was given freely. Things only happen when you make them happen.

"The storm is only for a season," said the preacher. "Don't forget to pray, my brothers and sisters."

"Yes, brother," the passengers agreed.

The bus was approaching 135th street, and Jeffrey looked out the window again. This time he saw a sign that read: Welcome to Opa Locka. He was ready to get off, so he pressed the buzzer.

"Stop requested," said the recorded voice from the bus speakers, and then the driver pulled up to the bus stop.

The man was still preaching while Jeffrey was getting off. "Just keep on holding on, beautiful people. The darkest part of the night is right before the morning rise," said the man with a smile.

Jeffrey and the preacher made eye contact before he exited the bus, and the man's look gave him a sense of confidence. However, he did not quite understand the man's message, just like he did not understand anything else happening in his life, like the drastic changes.

Chapter 5

One year later, and Little Jeff was still in Opa Locka. He still had no place to call home, but he felt most comfortable in that little city compared to everywhere else he went. By 18 years old, he had grown a couple inches taller, though he had lost a few pounds. His lowcut grew into a nappy afro, and he was starting to grow a beard; his demeanor was rather unfriendly. Eventually, he realized that being homeless was far tougher than working to pay bills.

Nevertheless, he came across a few street hustlers while he was out there, and they showed him different schemes to make money. He caught on quickly and even learned how to talk the Miami street slang. His life was a day-to-day survival story, which meant taking risks and worrying little about the consequences. He had to be a wolf and not a sheep to make ends meet, but still, most of his questions remained unanswered. Since that Friday, he had not been back to SAM'S grocery store a year ago when he was evicted. After he lost his mother's house, he did not see the purpose of going. Instead of working a regular job, he was turning to a life of crime, realizing that there were faster and sometimes much easier ways to get money.

Furthermore, with having no support or guidance, except for his mother's voice in his head, he would do anything for a profit besides selling his soul. He became fearless, and in terms of the street slang, he was hitting many licks, which meant to commit some type of crime to get a quick come up. His first real lick was to get a splack, another street term meaning stolen vehicle. The splack was for moving around under-the-radar, especially for late-night transportation, and it was also good to use to go on more licks. Whenever it gained too much attention, or in other words, got too hot, you were supposed to ditch it.

He often reflected on his life back in New Orleans. He thought about how if everything had remained the same, he would be graduating from high school right now, and his dad would be buying him his first car like he had promised. Jeffrey had been looking forward to that. Unfortunately, nothing was the same, and Jeffrey was left to figure life out on his own. He still wanted some wheels to maneuver with, but he was in no position to purchase one. Therefore, he was up early one morning, at nearby a gas station, lurking for a car to steal. Anyone careless enough to leave their keys in the ignition and go inside the store would be his victim. That morning, it was not long before a young lady driving a white Ford Focus pulled up and did that. She pulled up to a pump, exited the car, and ran inside the store without turning off the ignition. Jeffrey, who had watched her every move, eased his way up and glanced through the lightly tinted windows to make sure that no one else was in the car. Then, he pulled the door handle, hopped in quickly, drove off in a hurry, and got missing.

Jeffrey was stuck in a phase of uncertainty where day and night repeated themselves rapidly, and he yearned for stability. When Jeffrey got off the bus in Opa Locka a year ago, he walked down 135th street until he reached Pepper Park. He rested on a bench inside one of the dugouts; that was where he spent his first night and then most of his nights since. Besides the park, whenever he came across money from a lick that went well, he would rent a cheap motel room for as long as he could afford. Any other night, if he had a splack, he would park it somewhere safe, and then he would sleep right there in the car. Despite all that he was going through, he never lost his sanity, and he maintained his sense of humor along with his hope for better days.

One Saturday evening toward dusk, Jeffrey decided to drive to the corner store to pick up some snacks for the night. When he made it to the store, the clerk, an Arabic man, was the only one in there. He watched Jeffrey from the cameras as he floated up and down the aisles, looking for snacks. Minutes later, in came two hoodlums, dressed in all black clothing with hoodies and ski masks. They pulled out their guns and wasted no time getting down to business; it was a robbery, and Jeffrey was caught right in the middle of it.

The taller guy started giving orders. "Nobody fucking move!" he commanded while waving his gun around the store to check for customers. He was carrying a Glock 19 with a 32-round extension magazine, and his partner had a double barrel, sawed-off shotgun. After locking the door behind them, the shotgun man locked his aim in on the clerk's head. The taller one pointed his gun at Jeffrey, who was stuck in his tracks in one of the aisles.

"Let's make this really simple," he began. "You, little man, get on the ground and keep your face down," he instructed, and Jeffrey did what he said with no hesitation, trying to avoid all problems.

Then, the gangsters focused their attention on the clerk behind the register with his hands in the air, terrified. "Please, don't shoot. Take anything you want," the Arabic man pleaded.

"Do anything stupid, and that's your ass," said the man with the handgun. "Now, open the register and put everything on the counter!"

The clerk knew they were not bluffing. So he opened the register quickly and dumped all the cash on the counter. Without hesitating, the man in charge pulled a bag from his pocket and quickly scraped up all the money while his partner kept his aim steady on the clerk. From the floor, Jeffrey was crouched vigilantly, watching their every move.

"The safe too, Arab! Open the safe," the guy with the pistol yelled after he got all the register money into the bag. The Arabic man was hesitant. He gave them a perplexed look, wanting to say that there was no safe, but the shotgun man started moving in closer. Therefore, fearing for his life, the clerk bent down to open the safe, and when he looked up again, he was staring into the barrels of the shotgun.

"Bingo!" The gangsters shouted when the safe opened and they saw that it was full of money.

Then, they made the clerk go in a corner and turn his back, while the man in charge went behind the counter and took everything out of the safe. After that, they demanded he release the surveillance tape and gave him a gun-butt to his head for him to speed things up. The Arabic man was now bleeding, and he gave up the videotape while still begging for his life.

The robbers had gotten everything they were there for, and it was now time for them to head out. However, before they went out the door, the man with the handgun approached Jeffrey.

"Hey, shorty, what the fuck you peeping at?" he asked angrily.

Jeffrey was frightened, and he dropped his head quickly and put his hands up. "I didn't see anything. I promise," he yelled.

Then, suddenly the gunman's attitude changed as if something caught his attention. "Let me see that ring, shorty! Take it off," he reckoned.

Jeffrey was devastated because it was his father's pinky ring, the one with the diamond triangle, and it was special to him. However, his life was being threatened, so he figured it was time to let it go. Therefore, he took the ring off and handed it over to the gunman without even looking. Then, to his surprise, the guy looked at it for a second and then pitched it back to him.

"Hold on to that shorty," said the robber. Then he swung his gun back in the clerk's direction while maneuvering towards the door.

His partner continued to aim at the clerk until they signaled to each other that it was time to go. They unlocked the door and made their way out. There was a getaway car waiting around the corner for them, and they ran to it, got in, and eased off smoothly, leaving the scene uninterrupted. The clerk was still shaken up. He was furious; he went insane after the robbers left the store, swearing and cursing in a language that Jeffrey did not understand. Then, he fumbled around for his phone to call the police while Jeffrey took that time to ease his way out. He was a bit frightened, but knowing that he had a stolen car outside, he did not care to tarry inside the store.

Therefore, he left and drove a couple blocks over to a gas station and purchased his snacks from there. Then, while he was driving back towards Pepper Park, the details of the robbery replayed in his head. He thought about how unpredictable life could be, and then he decided that it was a good time to ditch the splack since he was sure that he had been seen on camera getting in and out of it. Therefore, he drove through one of the quieter neighborhoods of the city and found a dead-end street, where he parked it on the curb, wiped down everything that he had touched, and got out. Then, he ran full speed until he was far away from the vehicle, and then he started walking. He was about 20 minutes away from Pepper Park, and it was getting dark, so he decided to go there for the night to sleep in one of the dugouts.

Chapter 6

When Jeffrey arrived at the park, it was dark and gloomy, and there was no one in sight. He sat down on one of the benches to relax, and then, he used a back wood that he bought from the gas station to roll up some marijuana that he had. About three to four months earlier, he had picked up the habit of smoking. It was introduced to him by a street hustler, a.k.a. the weed man, who taught him how to roll it up and how to inhale it. Jeffrey tried it for himself, and he fell in love with the art. It was the only thing that took him away from his misery and numbed his pain. Therefore, he rolled his joint, lit up, and took a puff. After a few more puffs, the feeling started to kick in. While he sat there, he reflected on the robbery again and was impressed with how smoothly the gunmen operated. They were no amateurs. They did everything to the T and got the job done in roughly ten minutes; however, Jeffrey was unsure why that guy gave him his ring back. Moreover, he was high and did not want to puzzle his brain, so he disregarded the incident and continued to smoke to clear his mind.

A few minutes later, as Jeffrey sat there, slumped on the bleachers, high as a kite and drowsy at the same time, he heard music playing in the night's air. Heavy bass came from the vehicle's stereo as it drove slowly past the area where Jeffrey was lounging. The music was getting louder and louder, so he sat up straight to look around. He saw a navy-blue Thunderbird with dark tints heading towards him. He was now on high alert, and his eyes followed it as it continued slowly down the street with the music blasting. When the vehicle reached the stop sign at the end of the road, it stayed there for a while, which was unusual. Then surprisingly, the Thunderbird began to reverse.

"Oh, Lord, what now?" said Jeffrey, who figured that the driver of the vehicle was up to no good.

The Thunderbird came to a stop directly in front of Jeffrey, and again, it sat there for a while. It was rather spooky. Little Jeff was staring uncomfortably at the tinted windows that would not allow him to see past them when the driver's door opened. Out came a roughneck-looking guy with jailhouse muscles, about 6 feet and 3 inches tall, with a black-n-mild in his hand. He was wearing a black tank top with some baggy blue Girbaud jeans and black Reeboks.

He approached Jeffrey with a slight limp, and then, with the mug of a scare crow, he asked. "Who is you, lil nigga?"

Jeffrey noticed the pistol hanging out of the guy's pocket, and he stood up to face the pants sagging, gun slanging, goal teeth wearing gangster.

"What's up, boss? I don't want no problems," he replied. "I'm just chilling right now! My name is Jeffrey."

"Just chilling? On my turf, lil nigga?" he asked, as he stared Jeffrey up and down, with his top lip slightly lifted to the corner. "Oh, I see, you must don't know who the fuck I am!"

Jeffrey shook his head. "Nah, bro, I don't. I'm not from around here," he replied while staring the guy right in the eyes to show sincerity and a lack of intimidation.

"It's Opa Locka Bullet Head, motha fucka!" The guy yelled, and then he continued. "The name speaks for itself! I'm the city's finest, nigga!"

He was right because his name did ring a bell in Jeffrey's head, who had heard from many different people that this guy Bullet does not play. He is a cold-blooded murderer on the top of the cops' most wanted list, and there Jeffrey was, face to face with the man himself. His bald head was shaped like a bullet, so people called him Bullet Head, but most of the time, it was just Bullet for short, which was fitting for his criminal lifestyle.

"These are my streets," Bullet continued, "my neck-a-the-woods, and they're dangerous! So, give me one good reason why I shouldn't put my gun in your face right now!"

"Man, I ain't got nowhere to go, bra. I been catching hell lately," Jeffrey began. "A nigga killed my moms, and ever since then, I been out here!"

From school days back in Carol City, he had been hearing many stories about Bullet and his murderous gang, about them being responsible for most of the crimes in Dade County. Reflecting on his childhood, he had no idea that the day would come when he would be in the heart of the streets dealing with criminals. However, he figured that his honesty was his best way out.

"Look, Jit," Bullet began. Then he paused, and it seemed as if something interrupted his thought process. "Hold on, hell nah," he continued while pointing at Jeffrey and shaking his finger. "Boy, you do look familiar!"

Jeffrey smiled. "I don't know, but when my mom was murdered just about a year ago, it was aired on the news." Then, as he mentioned his mother, he became upset, and he continued. "Some punk robbed her for her purse and still shot her down in the process."

Bullet shook his head. "Oh shit!" he exclaimed. "I knew your ass looked familiar! Wasn't that homicide in Carol City?"

"Yeah, it was! You might have seen me on the news," Jeffrey replied.

Bullet found it amusing. "Sheesh, that's crazy! Hell yeah, that is exactly where I saw you at! So, that was your ol' girl that got killed?"

"Yes, sir," Jeffrey nodded. "She was all I had, bra, and I'll pay a fortune to find the fool who did it! I need to get that off my chest. You feel me?"

"Damn right, lil nigga, I feel you! Them lil petty thief ass niggas ain't have to kill her," Bullet replied. Then he paused for a second with a mysterious look on his face. "Now, what if I tell you that I know the clown who did it?" he asked.

And Jeffrey's countenance was immediately lit as his eyes opened wide. "Real talk, no bullshit?" he beckoned.

"Nigga, do you know who the fuck I am? If I say it's so, then it's so, my boy!" said Bullet, and Jeffrey nodded. "It's a nigga name Beans, from the Back Blues," he continued. "I don't fuck with that side at all, but them niggas know my legacy."

Jeffrey was fully energized. "Look, big homie, I need to see that fool, like a.s.a.p."

Bullet was intrigued with the sound of mischief, so he continued to stir it up. "Yeah, I bet," he replied. "Matter of fact, them fuck niggas should be out there hanging out as we speak."

Little Jeff had been waiting on this day for a year now, and he was ready to go. "Man, say less, pull me up, and the rest is history! You gotta do me this favor, big homie. I owe you one!"

"I believe we can work something out," said Bullet, who always had something up his sleeve. "In fact, one of my top shooters got killed recently in a gun battle, and I could use another young soldier on my team. So, depending on how you pull this off, I might just take you under my wings. You dig?"

"Hell yeah! Put the gun in my hand, and it's a wrap," said Jeffrey with confidence.

If you stand for nothing, you will fall for anything. Jeffrey was overlooking the fact that he was making a deal with a notorious gangster. However, he felt like he had nothing to lose since his life was filled with mere circumstances. For him, avenging his mother's death was his top priority, hoping that killing the man who was responsible would mend his broken heart. Therefore, he accepted Bullet Head's offer; it was an opportunity that he would not walk away from.

Bullet laughed a little, and then in a matter of seconds, he was back serious. "Don't worry, Jit, we got plenty guns! But please, understand what you get'n yourself into. I could tell that this will be your first body, but once you pull that trigger, it ain't no turning back."

Jeffrey wasn't really listening; his focus was set on facing his nemesis. "Man, let's do it! That fuck nigga gotta pay," he replied.

Bullet nodded. "Alright then, let's do it! But peep this, if you try anything slick, I will take your fucking head off," he warned him as they walked back to the Thunderbird.

"Man, it won't be no need for all that. I know what's going on," said Jeffrey, who knew better than to think that Bullet was bluffing.

"That's good! So, I guess we got us a deal then, J Boy." Bullet had already given him a nickname.

"Yes, sir! It's a deal," said Jeffrey as they got in the vehicle.

Then, when they sat down and closed the doors, Bullet took a 38-special from under his seat and handed it over. Then, he said calmly: "It's your world now, J Boy!"

Jeffrey held the revolver, and he stared at it graciously; it was the first time that someone had ever put a gun in his hand. Nevertheless, he gripped it like he had been a hitman for many years.

Bullet went on. "It's already loaded and ready for action. And there is a lot more where that came from. You smell me?"

Jeffrey smiled. "True story," he replied.

"Now, let's go spin a couple corners," said Bullet.

Then, the Thunderbird pulled off slowly into the still of the night, accelerating smoothly under the light of the moon. Indeed, death was lurking on that Saturday night as Bullet and Jeffrey drove towards the bloody mission.

Miguel Bash

Chapter 7

The Back Blues, where Beans lived, is the street name given to a run-down apartment complex on the west end of Opa Locka. Jeffrey was observant, paying attention to every detail as they arrived. He noticed the graffiti on the front wall of the yellow buildings that read: Murda Capital. The gate at the entrance was broken, leaving the complex open to any visitor. Therefore, the Thunderbird crept right through, and Bullet dimmed the lights and cracked the windows as he drove slowly. Jeffrey was silent but apprehensive, feeling the moment approaching when he would face his archenemy.

Bullet whispered. "J Boy, look if you see anybody hanging out."

"I'm already focused," Jeffrey replied.

As the T-Bird cruised around the loops of the buildings, they surveyed the area with wide-open eyes, looking for anything that was moving. Their surroundings were relatively quiet until they reached the last building in the very back of the complex. It was dark and creepy with three stories of apartments, a narrow road, and a high wall.

"Listen," said Jeffrey as he sat up. "I hear voices!"

Bullet stopped the car before they went down the narrow road, and they scanned the area to see what was happening. Three guys were hanging out by the stairways at the end of the building, drinking and smoking while laughing and chatting.

"Bingo!" said Bullet. "I knew them motha fuckas would be out," he continued. "There's your man, J Boy, the nigga with the red bandana.

That's Beans."

Immediately, Jeffrey went for the door to hop out, but Bullet stopped him. "Hold up, J Boy. Let's do it with style." Then, he put the transmission in reverse and backed into an empty parking space in the cut. "Creep up on them niggas and handle your business, then run back this way. I'll get us the fuck outta here," said Bullet.

"Say less!" Jeffrey replied.

Then, Jefferey got out of the vehicle and closed the door quietly. He crouched towards his nemesis, hiding behind the cars in the parking lot as he went down the lane. Bullet Head began to smile, watching from a distance; he was usually amused whenever someone was about to die. Jeffrey maneuvered nicely and smoothly down the dark road until he was one step away from where the three guys were hanging out. Now, he was able to hear them clearly, and they were still laughing and joking around. As he stopped to catch his breath, his trigger finger itched, and his adrenalin rushed. Then, he cocked the hammer, took a deep breath, and made his move.

Jeffrey popped out of the dark like a Jack-in-the-box, aiming his gun at the one with the red bandana. "Nobody fucking move!" said Jeffrey.

They were taken by surprise, but they still managed to get up and scatter like roaches. "Oh shit," they yelled simultaneously.

Then, one of them ran up the stairs, and the other two, including Beans, ran out towards the narrow road.

It was as if they were signing their death wish. Without ever dropping his aim, Jeffrey followed his target. He then opened fire just before Beans was able to run too far. He squeezed the trigger twice, letting off two shots, and the 38-special sang loudly, echoing in the night's air.

"Aw, damn! Fuck!" Beans cried after he caught a bullet in his leg and fell.

Jeffrey was a little surprised with his marksmanship; however, he was living the moment as he approached the crying bastard to finish him off. The other two guys kept running without even looking back. Now, he had the guy who killed his mother right where he needed him, under the barrel of his gun.

Sweat was dripping off Beans' face as he begged for mercy. "Alright! Alright! Anything you need, man! Please, just don't kill me!"

Jeffrey knelt and placed the revolver's barrel at Beans' temple, and then he whispered. "Don't you remember, fool? That lady you robbed and killed last year in Carol City? Well, that was my mother, you asshole!"

Beans eyes widened, and guilt was written all over his face. His body language was confirmation as he trembled with fear. "You got the wrong man! I swear," he pleaded.

However, there was no turning back. Jeffrey stared into the eyes of his long-sought rival and felt flashbacks of the pain he had faced over the past year. He reflected on the sight of his mother lying on the stretcher, wounded and bloody. He thought *this misery is just a squeeze away from being over with.* Nevertheless, he was hesitant until a voice in his head shouted: 'Shoot him,' and Little Jeff pulled the trigger once again. This time, the bullet landed in Beans' marrow and took his life.

Blood splashed on Jeffrey's clothes as he stood up and backed off. "Take that, you son of a bitch," he whispered to Beans, who lay lifeless.

Then, Jeffrey started to maneuver back towards the getaway car; he was sweating and breathing hard as he ran back up the dark road. Bullet, who had watched the whole thing, was impressed, but he was ready to go. The night was quiet, and the gunshots were sure to have alerted a few people. When Jeffrey made it back to the Thunderbird sweating bricks, his heart skipped a beat when he heard sirens nearby.

"Hell yeah, J Boy! You got that fuck nigga," said Bullet when Jeffrey got in the car.

When he caught his breath, Jeffrey nodded and replied. "Hell yeah! But let's slide! I hear 9 coming."

"Sit tight! I got this," said Bullet.

Jeffrey returned the murder weapon to Bullet, who was focused on making his way back towards the one-way in, one-way out apartment complex entrance. His headlights were now back on, and he drove as smoothly as possible. The reflections of red and blue lights were bouncing off visible objects as they got closer to the entrance. Bullet Head wanted to make it out the gate before the cops locked the place down, so he kept his cool and continued to push forward. However, when they came in clear view of the broken gate, they noticed a squad car making its way towards the back where they were coming from. Jeffrey was paranoid, and chills ran up his spine when he saw the car with flashing lights heading towards them. The officer who was driving saw the Thunderbird trying to make its way out and decided to stop them. Therefore, he swung his car a little to the left to block the road and placed his transmission in park. That maneuver caused Bullet to slam on his brakes and stop the vehicle. Then, with no questions asked, Jeffrey opened his door and jumped out.

"What the fuck are you doing?" Bullet yelled as the door slammed in his face.

Jeffrey then began to run back towards the rear of the apartment complex where Beans lay dead. With his head ducked down, he ran full speed until he bent his first corner, where Bullet and the cop were no longer visible. A little while after he bent the corner, he heard a gunshot, which stopped him in his tracks when it echoed. He thought he was hit and began to check himself for a wound, but he was good. Then he realized that the sound had come from around the corner, where Bullet and the cop were held up. Therefore, he continued to run, trying to get as far as possible away from the scene. He wondered what might have happened to Bullet, but he was more focused on his own well-being; he figured that he had the leeway and a little time to escape.

When he made it back to the last building in the complex, separated by the narrow road and the high wall, he stopped and knelt in a cut to catch his breath. Then, he checked his surroundings to make sure that no one was watching him. Many people were coming out of their apartments to see what was happening. He realized the high wall in the back of the complex was his only way out and analyzed how he would attack it. He saw a big dumpster close to the wall, and he figured that he would run and jump on that to get a boost, and then from there, he would jump and hopefully catch and grip the top of the wall. It was do or die, and he only had one chance; as he contemplated, he heard sirens drawing near to the back, and he felt the incoming pressure. The cops followed directly behind him after getting the heads up that one of the suspects was on foot.

Jeffrey decided that it was time to attempt the jump, and therefore, he executed it exactly how he planned. He ran from where he was hiding and jumped up on top of the dumpster. Then, with all his strength, he leaped towards the high wall, and luckily, he grabbed and gripped it. Then, with his upper body strength, he pulled himself up, as people who noticed him began to point and yell. The cops rushed the lane in time to see his legs dangling as he made his way over the wall. Then, Jeffrey jumped down to the other side without hesitating, crashing to the ground as he landed. He was bruised up, but he managed to get back up on his feet and keep going. The cops scrambled up and down the narrow road like headless chickens, daring to attempt the jump, which seemed like it was almost impossible. They got on their radios requesting backup and giving information about a suspect on the loose in the area adjacent to the apartment complex.

There were acres of grassy land behind the Back Blues where Jeffrey was on the move, continuously running without looking back. The police force was setting up a perimeter around the area, doing everything in their power to apprehend the murder suspect. As Jeffrey was trying to move faster than lighting, he approached another residential area. Many discomforting thoughts were flashing through his mind as he ran, and he dreaded the idea of getting caught. However, he made it to the residential neighborhood, jumped over a short wire fence, and found himself in someone's backyard. Minutes later, as he analyzed his surroundings, two ferocious Bulldogs came from around the side of the house, growling with their mouths dripping.

"Oh shit!" Jeffrey mumbled.

Then, the dogs rushed and attacked him while he kicked wildly at their mouths, maneuvering towards the side fence. His legs were scratched up from their teeth, but he managed to get away and jump over the fence to the neighboring backyard. There, he rested for a minute and watched the dogs as they continued to bark and tug on the fence. He did not want to alert the people in the houses, who were probably sleeping, and therefore, he got up and kept moving. The cops had no idea where he was, but they were close, and they were not going to give up the search.

Jeffrey was starting to realize that killing Beans did not make things any better. It only opened doors for more trouble. He forgot all about Bullet and the deal that they made, which had already gone bad. He was in the heat of the moment. Sirens filled the distant air, and everything else was irrelevant besides escaping. His life and freedom were both on the line, and it was a gamble that he was not ready to make. Therefore, he went from backyard to backyard. He had the darkness of the night to his advantage. So, he ran at top speed, moving on absolute adrenaline.

Chapter 8

Jeffrey was aware of the harassment that would follow if he were to get caught. In fact, he thought that the cops would kill him. It was going on two o'clock in the morning. The search, during which Jeffrey would hide somewhere for a while and then move again, when necessary, had been going on for over an hour. He had heard many unpleasant stories about prison in the past and was certain that such a place would drive him insane. These thoughts and many more were bouncing around in his head as he evaded the force. Unfortunately, he was yet to find safety. He was nearly exhausted; however, the heat was still on. He had run so many miles that he had made it back to 135th street, which was sort of familiar. Therefore, he ran eastwards towards Pepper Park, which was on 12th avenue. The cops were having trouble finding him because it was dark. Plus, he avoided the main roads, running through alleys and backyards, jumping over gates and fences.

After running a few blocks eastward, Jeffrey found himself between 22nd and 17th avenues. He decided to cross over on the north side of 135th street. Two squad cars patrolled down 22nd Avenue, and he caught a glimpse of them as he hurried across the street. When he made it to the other side, he saw some buildings that looked like small warehouses and figured he could hide there for a while since he really needed rest and could not go much further. He was not sure if the cops saw him or not, but he wanted to get off the scene, and so, he used his last bit of strength to run and jump over the wall that surrounded the small warehouse buildings. The wall was about half the size of the one in the Back Blues, and when he landed, he tried to get up and stand, but he was unable to move; his legs were powerless, and he was dehydrated.

The cops he saw strolling down 22nd Avenue spotted someone, but they could not really tell who it was, so they called for backup as they made U-turns to check it out. Jeffrey was laid out on his back behind one of the small buildings, gasping for air; his energy was drained, and his head felt like it was about to lift off. However, the police continued to apply the pressure. Now, about six squad cars were circling around the area of 135th street. He was able to see the reflections of their lights bouncing off the wall of the building where he lay. Therefore, mentally he began to prepare himself for the worst, worrying that they would soon find him and arrest him. Tears began to flow from his eyes as he looked up at the constellations feeling completely helpless. Then, suddenly he remembered the man preaching on the bus, the day when he left Carol City. The man's voice replayed in his head with words of encouragement.

"Don't forget to pray, my brothers and sisters," said the voice.

Jeffrey took heed, and he whispered. "Lord, please have mercy!"

Then, minutes later, as he lay there crying amidst the darkness, out of nowhere, there was light. The back door of the building opened slowly, and out came an elderly man whistling softly in the heat of the night. The man was carrying cardboard boxes that he had broken down. That was when he saw the injured lad laid out in the back of his building. He was so frightened when he saw Jeffrey that he threw the boxes and jumped back.

"Wow! Man, who is you?" the man yelled.

"Please, help me," said Jeffrey, who was still crying.

Then, the man asked a series of questions with a sense of concern.

"What's going on? Are you ok? How did you get back here?"

"I jumped the wall," Jeffrey panted. "Man, I'm in pain, and the cops are trying to kill me!"

"Is that why all these sirens around here? What did you do?" The man asked as he approached the feeble lad to help him to his feet.

"Sir, it's a long story," said Jeffrey. "But please, don't let them find me," he begged desperately.

"Don't worry, come with me," the old man replied calmly. Then he helped little Jeffrey into the building.

Jeffrey was a pitiful sight. There, at the edge of doom and in the mix of the madness, appeared this elderly man with compassion in his eyes in the nick a time. The man had observed him with much skepticism, but there was also courage in the man's eyes. Jeffrey himself was never the type to trust anyone too soon, but at that point, he was choiceless. Moreover, the old man's energy was that of an angel, and Little Jeff felt like his prayer was answered.

"Sir, thank you so much," said Jeffrey sincerely.

He was still trying to catch his breath while limping his way into the building. The man disregarded his duty with the cardboard boxes and served as a crutch to the helpless stranger. Then, when they made it inside, he locked the doors and turned off the lights.

"Follow me," said the elder.

They tiptoed quietly towards the front of the building to get a peep through the window. They were frightened to see that the red and blue lights were in the parking lot. The cops were circling the warehouse buildings, not quite sure if their suspect was hiding or still on the move. A few of them were even on foot with their flashlights walking around checking under cars.

Jeffrey crossed his fingers and begged within. "Lord, please don't let them come to this door."

Nevertheless, it was doubtful that they would since no one expected anyone to be in any of the buildings at that time of night. Therefore, the cops were more focused on the outdoors.

"Man, you must have been running really fast," the man

whispered. "Because I don't think they know where you are!"

Jeffrey smiled. "I was running faster than I ever did!" he replied as they continued to watch.

The cops were walking around clueless, talking, and pointing in different directions. The only description they had for the suspect was a young black male dressed in black clothing. About 30 minutes passed. Then, amidst their scrambling around, a message from a higher-up came in on one of their walkie-talkies. It appeared urgent because the policemen raced back to their vehicles, jumped in, and slammed the doors. Then, the tires screamed as they peeled off, rushing out of the parking lot as if the message was about the president.

"Wow!" Jeffrey sighed with relief. "They really do not know where I am."

"Yeah, maybe they saw someone else who fit the description," the elder replied as they watched the cops rush out.

Within the next five minutes, the area was clear of all police. After those nerve-wracking hours, Jeffrey finally began to gain some reassurance. He logically thought his life would be over while he was pursued but kept moving even though he did not see a way out. Now, his conscience was raging with guilt for taking another man's life, which was certainly not the feeling that he expected after avenging his mother's death. Mentally, he was beating himself up, wishing that everything would have gone differently. He felt condemned like a wasted effort, the picture of sin.

It took about another hour after the cops left before Jeffrey was assured that he had escaped. Then, he took a break from peeping out the window and checking the outskirts. It was dark, so the elderly man turned on a small lamp to keep the brightness minimal. Jeffrey began to look around and observe; he noticed a digital clock that read, 4:00 a.m. He also saw a plaque on the wall near where he was standing, an appreciation award for Bobby's Meals. The old man went to a Pepsi cooler in the building, fetched two bottles of water, and handed one to

Jeffrey.

"Here's some water," said the elder.

"Thank you, sir! I needed that," Jeffrey replied, and then he stooped down and sat in a corner on the floor to drink it.

"My name is Bobby King. Folks call me Bob," said the man. He had long dreadlocks and a full-grown beard of hair that was mostly grey.

"Very nice to meet you, sir," Jeffrey replied as he reached up to shake the man's hand. "Man, you saved my life! I don't know how to thank you," he emphasized.

The man smiled. "Don't worry yourself. What is your name?" he asked.

"My name is Jeffrey, Jeffrey Jacob."

"Nice to meet you, Jeffrey," said the elder. "Now, tell me, why were you running from the police? And why you have blood all over your clothes?"

The questions triggered some flashbacks in Jeffrey's mind, and the room was silent for a moment as he reminisced. Then, tears began to flow from his eyes, and he cried. "Man, I killed him. I can't believe I killed him," said Jeffrey.

"Wait! What? Who did you kill?" asked the man, who was now perplexed.

Jeffrey looked at him with tearful eyes, and he replied. "The man who murdered my mother. Sir, it's a long story."

The elder was shocked by that response, but he saw that the young man was vulnerable. Therefore, he assured him: "Right now, we have nothing but time! You can tell me all about it, son."

However, Jeffrey's mind was being tormented by replays of the recent homicide. Again, he was able to see Beans' pitiful face as he begged for mercy. Then, the sound of the gunshots that he fired echoed in his head, and he remembered Beans brains splashing out after he fired the last shot to seal the deal. He lowered his head with shame, clueless about how to go forward with his life. He could have never imagined playing with a real gun back in his childhood, not to mention taking another man's life. Therefore, instantly his thoughts became suicidal. As they drove him insane, he viciously aroused from the floor to find a knife or any other sharp object to kill himself.

Then, he saw a large flathead screwdriver laying around, and he went for it.

"I'm just going to put an end to all this misery," he cried.

Bobby King, who was paying close attention, leaped like a tiger and tackled the troubled child, a move that caused the screwdriver to fall from Jeffrey's hand. It echoed when it hit the concrete.

"Calm yourself down! There won't be any suicides in here tonight," Bob yelled sternly while maintaining the restraint.

They were both on the ground, breathing heavily until Jeffrey came to his senses and convinced the old man that he would not hurt himself. Mr. King's strength was proven, with a firm grip for his age, and he demonstrated that he was ready for the unexpected.

"Just breathe. Inhale deeply! You are safe now! Free yourself by expressing yourself. And tell me your story. I'm here to listen," said Bob.

Jeffrey did calm down eventually. When he caught his breath, he gathered the strength to tell Bob his life story. "Well, let me take you back to the beginning."

He was surprised to find someone who genuinely cared to listen, and therefore, he decided to not hold back any details. Starting from his childhood days in New Orleans, he spoke about how good his life was around that time. When his mother and his father were alive, it was the best time of his life. Then, he went on to tell the elder how drastically everything changed. How, first his dad got caught up in the street life, which ended him and his crew in a crashing collision. Then, he explained how things got tough for his mother, causing them to downgrade their lifestyle and eventually move to Miami.

Bob listened carefully, without missing a beat; he was compassionate about the situation that showed up at his doorstep. Jeffrey gave his mother credit for almost everything he knew and for instilling in him virtues like discipline, politeness, responsibility, and contentment. He spoke of the tragedy of his mother being robbed and killed at the bus stop one evening on her way home from work.

"Man, I'm so sorry to hear that," Bob interrupted as he shook his head.

And Jeffrey continued, telling the elder how reckless his life had become since then, finding himself stuck in a place where he knew nothing and no one. He mentioned his attempt to maintain the bills by working at SAM'S and the eviction that followed; then, he explained everything he experienced over the past year. He spoke about how he felt like he had nothing left to live for, nothing to lose, and the urge for revenge; then he included meeting Bullet and their bloody mission.

"So, here I am today, guilty of murder," he concluded.

Again, tears flowed from his eyes as he thought about everything, but he did feel a sense of relief from expressing himself. Bobby King was fighting to hold his own tears back as he soaked it all in; he had never heard a story from a teenager that was so intense. Furthermore, he was intrigued, and he considered it a duty to help the young man straighten his life out. Somehow, Bob felt like Jeffrey's pain was his own, and he was spiritually motivated to assist in any way possible. Therefore, he began with some words of encouragement, words that Jeffrey had never forgotten.

"First, you must ask God for forgiveness, and then you must forgive yourself," said Bob.

"Can I pray right now?" Jeffrey asked.

"Sure, let's pray together!" Bob replied.

So, they prayed together, and Jeffrey asked God to forgive him for all his sins. Then, when they were done praying, Bob continued to share his wisdom, with words that opened Little Jeff's eyes and gave him the inspiration he needed to rise again.

"Listen, son, in all that you do, you must remain conscious of the consciousness that is within you," said Bob.

Chapter 9

Two weeks passed, and Jeffrey remained a free man. He did his best to stay under the radar even though the cops never did get a good look at his face. If he were to walk past any of them, he probably would not be recognized. However, he kept a low profile and tried to not do too much moving around. He learned that the warehouse that he and the elder occupied that night was not just some old building. Each of the small buildings housed a business, mostly mechanic shops. They were in a well-known vegetarian restaurant, Bobby's Meals: Eat Smart, Think Smart. The elder had been there late to go over inventory, which he did when he was too busy to get it done. He was the proud owner and the chef of the small family business; moreover, his cooking style stood out amongst many. It was not long before Jeffrey fell in love with Bob's cooking. He was astonished to know that the restaurant had been there all along, so close to where he had lived for over a year, and he knew nothing about it.

Bob offered Jeffrey a position for assistance in the kitchen, with a starting pay of $500 every week. Jeffrey gladly accepted it. He needed something to keep him occupied; the offer was a no-brainer. Since his mother died, he had not met anyone who genuinely cared and wanted to see him do better. Bobby King was a lifesaver. All he wanted was to help to keep Little Jeff off the streets. The job was easy compared to working at SAM'S because the rest of the day went by relatively smoothly after the prepping was done in the mornings.

Jeffrey was lodging at a nearby motel, which he was renting at

the weekly rate of $300. From there, he was at the restaurant Tuesdays through Saturdays every week. He closed the curtains on his previous lifestyle, which consisted of burglarizing and carjacking. Now, his desire was to stick close to the wise man. Bob found pleasure in teaching, especially to those who were receptive. Bob taught Jeffrey priceless lessons about eating healthy, spiritual awareness, and living a clean and balanced lifestyle. He always said that those things were the keys to longevity, which he would know since he was 75 years old and was still strong.

The year 2007 ended, and Jeffrey was invited to the Kings' family house for New Year's Eve dinner and bringing in the New Year. The visit to their house was splendid; the atmosphere was warm and refreshing, Jeffrey felt like he was around his own family. He met Ziona, Bob's wife, and his two children, Jahfari and Makyah; he also met some other lovely relatives. Everyone's energy was positive, and Jeffrey was at peace with himself for the first time in a long time. He was revitalized and ready to turn a new page in his life.

Indeed, it was a Happy New Year. January 1, 2008, fell on a Monday, and Jeffrey was up and out early that morning. He had changed his look recently, from a nappy afro to a clean lowcut. He also professionalized his attire, the best way possible with what he could afford. The first thing on his agenda for that day was to go to the bank and open a new account to officially start saving his money. Therefore, he rode the 27A bus down to 79th street in Liberty City, where a few major banks and other businesses were located.

That morning, he was feeling like a bird spreading its wings over the horizon. He gave thanks to God in his head as he sat on the bus, expressing gratitude for divine guidance and protection throughout all his endeavors. Then, when the bus reached 79th street, he requested a stop, and when he got off it, he immediately saw a Wells Fargo bank. Therefore, he decided that he would open his first bank account with Wells Fargo.

When he entered the bank, it was quiet because they had just

opened about an hour earlier. There were only three people in line for the teller. He looked for someone to assist him, and momentarily, a professionally dressed woman walked up to him.

"Good morning, sir. What can I help you with today?" she asked.

"Yes, ma'am, good morning. I want to open a new bank account," Jeffrey replied.

"Oh, that is great," said the banker. "Well, thank you for choosing Wells Fargo. Just have a seat over there on the couch, and someone will be with you shortly."

"Ok, thank you," said Jeffrey with a smile.

While Jeffrey waited, he observed and soaked up the atmosphere of the professional setting. He had been interested in corporate issues and was exceptionally good with numbers as far back as he could remember. He often caught himself daydreaming about his future, hoping that he will own his own business one day. He was confident in believing that those dreams will soon become his reality. His mind drifted until he was gladly interrupted by the young lady who showed up to assist him. She was adorable, and Jeffrey felt an instant connection as he stood up to greet her; it was like love at first sight.

"Hello, good morning! My name is Jane, and I will be assisting you with opening your account today," said the young lady.

Jeffrey shook her hand gently. "That's wonderful! It's a pleasure to meet you," he replied.

She smiled. "Likewise. Right this way," said Jane, as she led him to her desk.

Jeffrey was checking her out as he followed her, admiring her beauty and elegance. Her brown skin was spotless, and her hair was neatly done in stylish kinky twists that dropped down a little past her shoulders. Her desk was in the corner of the room near a window that allowed the sunlight to beam through. When they sat down, she went over a few basic things required to open his checking account. The sunlight and her personality had the room lit as she collected his personal information. They were both glowing, and her responses gave him a hint that she was not stuck up but relatively open-minded. Therefore, he could not resist the urge to pursue her. So, he took his shot.

"Honestly, Jane, you are the prettiest girl that I ever seen," said Jeffrey.

"Really?" Jane blushed. "Well, thank you, Mr. Jeffrey," she replied, showing off her dimples.

As he looked in her eyes, he fantasized, drawn in by her attraction, and the chemistry between them was indeed alive. He went on. "So, do you like working here?"

"Yes, sir! This is my dream career," she replied as she continued to work on his profile. "Right now, I'm doing an internship because I am still in college."

Jeffrey was surprised to know that she was an intern because her professionalism gave him the impression that she had been there for a few years. "Well, you are doing a splendid job," he complimented. "You know, later when I look back at my day, this moment will be the highlight of it."

"You are such a sweetheart," Jane replied, blushing as she participated in the flirtation.

Then, after she completed his profile, they went to the ATM to activate his new temporary card by making a deposit. He started with a hundred dollars deposit; however, to him, it felt like a thousand. Bob had already given him permission to use the restaurant's address for anything he needed to receive. Therefore, he used it to receive his permanent card in the mail. His day was wonderful, especially since his meeting Jane, and he was excited about his new bank account.

When they got back to her desk to wrap it all up, he asked: "So, can I call you sometime?"

"Sure," she replied and handed him a card from her desk. "Here's my business card."

Jeffrey took it and smiled. "Thank you, but I mean like, off the record," he specified.

"Yes, my cellphone number is on there as well," she replied.

"Well, then," said Jeffrey, as he placed the business card and the bank card in his wallet. "Again, it was a pleasure. And I hope you have a wonderful rest of your day."

Jane was flattered, and she replied. "Thank you, honey. Have a great day!"

Then, Jeffrey took the envelope with his welcome kit and walked out feeling like a winner.

"Have a nice day, sir! Thank you for coming in," said the lady who greeted him when he walked in.

"Likewise," Jeffrey replied as he went through the doors.

Chapter 10

He was back in the busy environment of Liberty City. Outside the bank was a different world, more ghetto than professional. As he walked through the plaza past Citi Trend towards the Flea Market, he could not stop thinking about Jane. It had been a long time since he courted a female. He had never been in love, only a crush or two, in school back in New Orleans.

Nevertheless, Jeffrey was pleased with his performance that morning, seeing that apparently, he still had the juice. He decided to walk through Liberty Flea Market to pick up some T-shirts or whatever else he could afford. He was filled with gratitude as he entered the Flea Market, passed the barbershops at the entrance, and continued down the aisle in a buoyant mood. Suddenly, he stopped in his tracks while he was passing the first jewelry booth. The many encrusted diamonds glaring from the showcase immediately pulled him in like a magnet. He knew that he could not afford the cheapest thing in that booth; however, he still wanted to look, so he did.

"Can I show you anything?" the jeweler asked after noticing him staring at the pieces.

"No, thank you. I'm just looking," Jeffrey replied, not wanting to waste the man's time.

"Ok, let me know if you need my help with anything," said the jeweler.

"As a matter of fact, how much will it cost to clean this ring?"

Jeffrey asked as he removed his father's pinky ring from his finger.

"Ahh, just give me five bucks, and I will clean it up nice for you," the jeweler replied.

"Sounds good, let's do it," said Jeffrey as he handed the ring to the jeweler.

"Cool, give me about five to ten minutes," the jeweler replied, and then he walked over to the cleaning station.

Jeffrey continued to check out the various pieces they sold, chains, pendants, bracelets, watches, and rings. Then, while he was window shopping, he heard someone calling his name.

"Lil Jeff! Yoo! What's good?" said the voice that he heard, and it sure sounded familiar.

When he looked around, he saw a tall guy approaching him fast with a wide grin. "It's me, youngblood, Og Boe," said the guy excitingly.

Jeffrey could not believe his eyes when he realized that it was indeed his father's right-hand man. "No way! Og triple Og! What's good?" he replied with a burst of excitement. They hugged each other and laughed, and then Jeffrey continued. "Wait, I thought you was..."

"I know. Locked up or dead," Boe interrupted. "Let us talk about that later. How is your mother?" he asked.

"Man, she was murdered about a year and a half ago," Jeffrey replied. "I guess we can talk about that one later as well."

"Say what?" Boe exclaimed with a perplexed look. That answer was the last thing that he was expecting. "That is crazy! Yeah, let's talk about that when we get out of here."

"Say less! Man, I'm so glad to see you," Jeffrey emphasized.

"I'm glad to see you too, young star! I been trying to find you, ever since I knew you was in Miami," said Boe.

"For real? How did you know, and how did you find me?" Jeffrey asked.

Boe smiled. "Well, it was not so difficult. I just followed that ring right there," he replied while pointing at the ring that the jeweler was handing back to Jeffrey. Then, he continued. "Did you know that I was with your father the day when he bought that ring? It was nice then, and it is nice now. Jimmy couldn't resist it," said Boe, laughing as he reminisced.

Jeffrey laughed as he brandished the ring, which was glistening. "Wow! I did not know that," he replied as he gave the jeweler $5 for his service and then put the ring back on his finger.

"What you getting into today?" Boe asked, and then he went on before Jeffrey could give an answer. "I'm fixing to head to the crib to eat lunch. My girl is there cooking. You should come along with me so we can chop it up."

"Most definitely, Og. I'm with that," Jeffrey replied. "It's my day off today. I wasn't doing much, just hanging out."

"Perfect then, let's slide," said Boe.

Jeffrey felt good being with someone he knew from back home, a close friend of his family. He felt safe. They walked out of the Flea Market together and got into Og Boe's black Monte Carlo. Boe pulled out of the parking lot smoothly and then drove to his apartment building, which was only a few blocks over.

While they were in the car, Jeffrey asked. "Hey, Og, you said you followed the ring. What did you mean?"

Boe smiled. Then he looked at Jeffrey and said, "Let me take you back for a minute. Do you remember being on the scene of a robbery in a corner store in Opa Locka just a few weeks ago?"

The incident replayed in Jeffrey's mind as vividly as if it were yesterday. "As a matter of fact, I do! Wait," said Jeffrey as he processed his thoughts. "Were you there? Were you that guy who gave me my ring back?"

"Bingo!" Boe replied as he giggled. "I couldn't say much to you then, but that's when I knew you was in Miami, and I been trying to find you ever since."

"Man, that's crazy! I could not figure out why that man gave me my ring back, but now I see," said Jeffrey, and then he laughed. "Anyhow, I'm just glad that we are back in touch," he concluded.

"No doubt, Lil Jeff, I'm glad too," said Boe.

With the bending of a couple corners and a brief conversation, they were pulling into Boe's apartment building, which was only about 10 minutes away from the Flea Market. They got out of the car and walked up the stairs to the second floor, where Boe's apartment was.

"I got some exotic shit for you later to ease your mind," said Boe as they made their way to his apartment.

"That sounds like a plan," Jeffrey replied.

Then, Boe stopped at apartment number 214, and then he reached in his pocket for his keys. He opened the door, and they went in, and Jeffrey was impressed with the setup. The furniture and the décors were high quality and stylish. Overall, the apartment was clean, and it had a pleasant smell.

"Hey, Babes, we got company!" Boe yelled to his girlfriend, who came from the bedroom, lightly dressed in her house attire. "You won't believe who this is," he continued.

"Who is it?" she asked.

"This is my right-hand man Jimmy One-Shot's only son, Lil Jeff," he replied excitingly.

"Really? How did you find him?" His girlfriend asked curiously.

"I ran into him at the Flea Market," said Boe.

"Oh, that's great! How are you, sweetie? I'm Anna," said Boe's girlfriend to Jeffrey as she reached out for a handshake.

"It's a pleasure to meet you, Anna," Jeffery replied and shook her hand.

"Likewise! Boe always tell me stories about him and your father. Well, make yourself at home, and I hope you guys are hungry. The food is ready," said Anna.

"Yes, ma'am! Thanks much," Jeffrey replied.

Anna was a cute white girl with a nice petite body, the complete package, a girl who would literally do anything for Og Boe; she seemed like a cool person and a fun girl. The couple hugged and kissed each other, and then Anna went to the kitchen to fix the plates. She cooked baked chicken, garlic potatoes, and steamed broccoli, and it smelled good.

"Please, you guys enjoy," said Anna, as she laid their plates on the dining table. Then, she continued. "I will let you guys eat, and I'm sure that y'all have some catching up to do. So, honey, I'll be in the room if you need me."

"Ok, sweetheart," Boe replied as his girl made her way back to the bedroom.

Then, Boe and Jeffrey began to dig into their plates, and after a few minutes, Boe could not help but ask him. "Man, what on earth happened to your mom?"

Jeffrey kissed his teeth as he looked up from his plate. "Man, she was coming home from work one evening, and when she got off the bus, some trigger-happy fool ran down on her, held her at gunpoint, and robbed her. He snatched her purse, and then, he still shot her twice and killed her."

Boe slapped the table. "Bullshit!" he yelled. "Who the fuck did that?"

"Don't worry, Og. I already handled it," Jeffrey replied.

"Word?"

"Man, but I been catching hell since she died."

"I can only imagine, young soldier!"

They picked up where they left off on the plates, and Anna's cooking was speaking for itself. Boe began to reminisce as he ate, thinking about how the last time he saw Jeffrey in New Orleans. He was just an intelligent kid who had all the gadgets that every other kid wanted. Boe knew that the kid had grown into a man who had already been through more than the average person. It was a great link-up, and Jeffrey had many questions to ask because he wanted to know more about his father.

When they were done eating, they went and sat in the living room on the couch, and then, Og Boe pulled out an ounce of Og Kush. After letting Jeffrey smell it, he rolled up two fat joints and then passed one to Little Jeff. Boe was troubled within from the news that he heard about Ms. Elaine, and he really needed to calm his nerves. Therefore, they lit up the joints and began to puff, and it was not long before their heads were in the clouds. The Kush was some of California's finest, and as they puffed smoke, they were getting high as a kite.

"Hey Og, tell me about that day when my father died. I heard that y'all crashed, and you went to jail."

"Yeah, that is right, Lil Jeff, about that: I was with your dad, the day when he died, may his soul rest in peace. Boy, we had the cops on one of the longest and craziest chases in New Orleans history! Unfortunately, it turned out bad because we wrecked out. We could have all died, but I ended up being the only survivor. Shit, them folks sentenced me to life in prison," said Boe as he shook his head.

"That is crazy! So, how did you escape that?" Jeffrey asked.

"When I went to the camp, I settled in, and it was a good thing that I was around people who I knew from the outside. My respect was major because the Triple Beam's legacy was talked about in prison as much as it was in the streets. Anyways, I did about six years, and for most of that time, I was working as a trustee. While I was doing trustee work, I was paying attention to all the glitches and the loopholes in the system. Furthermore, I was part of a group of inmates that they allowed outside of the fences to work on a clean-up project. To make a long story short, one day, while I was out there, I saw an opportunity to escape, and I took it without second-guessing. Anna was already on standby, so I let her meet me at a certain location, and from there, we drove straight here to Miami. I been here on the run ever since," said Boe.

"Wow! Salute to you, Og. I'm glad that I get a chance to vibe with you years later."

"Hell yeah, this is dope! Man, even though I'm on the run, I been stacking up my paper. I have some major connections down here in Miami! You feel me?"

"Yes, sir, that's live!"

They were silent for a couple minutes as they continued to smoke, and the only sounds that were heard were from inhaling and exhaling. Little Jeff was relaxing with a gangster veteran, and it made him feel carefree and even gave him peace of mind.

"Please, tell me more about my dad," said Jeffrey.

Boe smiled and took another puff, then he began: "I remember, it was me, One-Shot, and Ramon Dollars - the Triple Beam Gang, baby! We were kicking up dust and making the most noise in the streets of New Orleans. Yeah, we were superstars in our ward, feared by our rivals, but respected by everyone. Man, no one was fucking with us! But the real brains behind our operation was your dad, Jimmy "One-Shot" Jacob; he was the organizer of the organization. I ain't never met anyone else with such ambition and loyalty. At the same time, to our enemies, he was a nightmare. Man, he did not fuck around. Even though the streets were on fire around that time, we had the money flowing in like clockwork. I respect your old man to the fullest. That's my big homie, even in his grave. Oh yeah, he always told me to keep an eye on you. So, I got you!"

Jeffrey was grateful to get a view of his father from a different perspective, and therefore, he was all ears. Some of the decisions he made in his life were starting to make more sense to him, as he noticed some traits in his bloodline. He smoked his joint down to a clip, and then he put out the fire, feeling good and relaxed.

"Man, I miss my dad so much!"

"I already know! Man, that day turned out to be the worst day of my life. Nothing has been the same since I lost my partners. That brinks truck job was either going to make us or break us, and it surely broke us. All I remember is the car flipping over and landing upside down."

They shook their heads at the same time and laid back on the couch. It was a healthy conversation, as Jeffrey continued to ask everything that he could think of. He also shared with Boe everything he had been through over the past few years, even before he and his mother left New Orleans. The Og was impressed with the little man's survival skills, and he assured him that they would stick together from that day forward.

"Well, mi casa es su casa," said Boe after they were done catching up. "I'm going in the room to chill out for a while. Make yourself at home, watch TV, or do whatever you want."

"Ok, big homie, I appreciate you," Jeffrey replied, and then Boe got up from the couch and went towards the bedroom.

Before he went in, he stopped and looked back. "Hey, Lil Jeff, I know you always had a way with words, and your rhymes were tight. You still doing your thing?" Boe asked.

Jeffrey smiled. "Well, not as much as I used to, but I still write from time to time to keep the fire burning."

"Ok, that's great! Don't stop writing. I know the perfect person to link you up with. This guy is big business. I will put together a meeting soon."

"Hell yeah, Og! I need that! Thanks again for everything."

"No sweat, I got you," Boe replied, and then he disappeared into the bedroom.

Jeffrey laid back on the couch and stared at the ceiling. He reflected on everything that he and Og Boe spoke about and everything that had happened that day. It was safe to say that it was a good day.

Miguel Bash

Chapter 11

The next day, Jeffrey was back at the restaurant, back and forth from the kitchen to the front counter, taking and serving orders. It was a busy afternoon with the waiting area filled with customers, who seemed talkative. Outside of the restaurant, the sun was blazing, and the world was moving at a fast pace; it was as if Bobby's Meals was some sort of headquarters. Bob's wife, Ziona, and his 31-year-old son, Jahfari, had stopped by for a couple hours. Elderly men in the waiting area were deep into an open conversation, mainly about rightful living and some of the issues that were happening in the world. Most of them were Bob's longtime friends, and such discussions were normal at the restaurant. The conversation was open to anyone who felt like sharing, and random people jumped in from time to time, including Bob and Ziona, who were also back and forth from the kitchen. However, Jeffrey was more focused on listening as he performed his duty to satisfy the customers. The knowledge from the elders was like music to his ears, being that most of what they were discussing were subjects that he never touched on. He was getting along well with Jahfari, who was helping in the kitchen, which allowed Bob to take a break. Therefore, Bob and his wife were in the front, entertaining the discussion.

"See, the thing is, life requires much discipline," said a Rastaman, who was drinking a natural carrot juice.

"Certainly, my brother!" Bob agreed. "Every man must strive to perfect that discipline."

"The teachings begin with us, the parents," Ziona added. "By educating and guiding the youths that they may become their best version."

Everyone gave their nod of approval, and then, another one of the elders jumped in: "Empress, that's absolutely true! We are the teachers, and the youths are the warriors. They must take a stand for what is right while they are still young."

The discussion went on in that manner as people came in and out of the restaurant. Some customers lingered and ate their food right there in the lobby to listen and participate in the discussion. Bobby's Meals, which had become the favorite restaurant for many people, has a unique menu. No meat, but you can get a Snapper fish, escovitch, or brown stew. Then, everything else is earth-grown, food that will not weigh you down. Bobby specialized in cooking tofu and veggie chunks in various flavors, rice and peas, and vegetables. Every day there was a different style along those same lines. Some days, you would discover sautéed ackee, okras, or sometimes sweet and sour flavor tofu on your plate. Usually, this is served with rice and peas, some greens, like callaloo or bok choy, and a piece of ground food, like yellow yam or green banana. Customers only had to specify whether they wanted a large or a small plate or to add a fish in the style of their preference to their meal. Besides that, there are various handmade natural juices on the menu, which were made by Ziona. The juices included: pine and ginger, carrot juice, sea moss, soy and grapefruit, and beetroot, just to name a few. The food quality was evident from the level of traffic in and out of the restaurant each day it was open. In fact, it was usually busy from the time it opened in the morning to when it closed in the evening; there was always at least one customer in there.

It was one of those days when most of everyone was in good spirits, feeding their stomachs and contributing to the ongoing discussion. Most of them were on their lunch breaks from near and far and ended up spending the entire time at the restaurant. Just as you can always expect some healthy food from Bobby's Meals, you can also expect some words of wisdom when you visit. The fanbase was international, and for many out-of-towners, it was mandatory to stop by whenever they were in Miami. The restaurant was the place to be, as the conversation continued.

"The way they designed the system is that the rich get richer, and the poor get poorer," said a random customer, who walked in and overheard the discussion. "Do you understand what we are up against? Or, better yet, the condition of our children's future?"

"Brother, I see the future being computerized," Bob replied.

Jeffrey found pleasure in serving the customers with food that they loved, and he was enjoying the day in his own way as he recorded the words of wisdom in his head. Spiritually, he was growing and moving gradually towards the path of enlightenment. After he began to look at the world differently, he noticed that many things were just illusions and plain vanity. Much credit was due to Bobby King making Jeffrey aware of what was truly valuable, being a father figure and a great role model. The elder led by example. He was a pioneer and a humanitarian who took the idea of upliftment and shaped it into a form that everyone could enjoy. Indeed, he was one of the cornerstones of the community, who was well known and respected; and his day-to-day mission was to properly serve the people

Unfortunately, on Ali Baba Avenue, Bullet Head and three of his soldiers were in the Thunderbird circling the area with cruel intentions. It was foggy behind the dark tints as they puffed marijuana smoke with each man carrying heavy artillery. They were in the act of searching around town for the missing youngster, who seemed to have gone incognito. Opa Locka's most wanted gangster was feeling truly disrespected. He had something that he wanted to get off his chest. In fact, he had been looking for Jeffrey ever since that night when Beans was murdered. He was furious, and his anger was boiling because no one ever played him and got away with it.

"Fuck! Man, where is this young nigga? You telling me that nobody seen this Jit?" Bullet asked, looking over at his homeboy, who was riding shotgun. The four gangsters were ready to jump out and make a mess.

"Nah, big bra! That lil nigga that you described is nowhere to be found," his homeboy Block replied.

"Boy, when I see that fuck nigga, that's his ass! Ya heard me?" Bullet exclaimed.

Flashback to that bloody Saturday night when the Thunderbird was cut off by the squad car. After blocking off the Thunderbird, the policeman got out of his vehicle. He approached the driver with his hand clutching his pistol. When Jeffrey jumped out and ran off, Bullet knew that using his gun was the only way out because going to jail was not an option for him. He had his favorite Glock 40 in his hand with one in the chamber ready to go. He waited until the policeman got close and gestured for him to get out of the vehicle, then slowly, he rolled his window down, far enough to shoot. One shot straight to the officer's head, and he collapsed; then, Bullet stepped on the gas and rammed into the squad car from an angle to push it out of his way. He managed to make it out of the one-way in, one-way out apartment complex in the nick-a-time before the other cops were able to block off the entrance.

The sound of the gunshot that stopped Jeffrey in his tracks that night while he was running came smoking from Bullet's Glock 40. Moreover, the two homicides in the Blues that night led the police force to a frenzy of rage. The apartment complex was put on lockdown, and the entrance was blocked off; no one was to enter or leave out. Also, many of the people who came outside to spectate were questioned and interrogated. Even though the Thunderbird slipped through the gates, it was spotted, and a couple of squad cars made U-turns and went after it. However, with a bit of leeway and an adrenaline rush, Bullet demonstrated his expertise behind the wheel. Being born and raised in that same city, he knew it well, which gave him somewhat of an advantage. He took his pursuers through different neighborhoods, around sharply bent corners, along many back roads. Then, when he got close to his neighborhood, he made a phone call to one of his partners and gave him instructions to open the gates in the back alley. The cops were still on him, but he had a nice gap that he used to make his escape. He turned down the alley leading to his partner's backyard and killed his lights immediately. Then, he drove smoothly through the gates that were already open for him, and his partner was there to close them quickly after the Thunderbird went through. It was a big backyard, so Bullet parked to the right side where the cops wouldn't see the car if they were to pass by. Then, he and his partner ran inside the house; it was a maneuver they had done a few times before. Not long after, one of the squad cars went down that same alley but passed right by the house, with no idea where the Thunderbird disappeared.

Bullet Head, who had all the advantages, managed to escape in the thick of the night. And though he was relieved, he realized how close he came to losing his freedom, which made him even angrier with Little Jeff. The cops were pissed off after realizing that they lost him, so they focused all their attention on the young man on foot. Two murders in one night, with no suspect in custody, the Opa Locka Police Force was truly upset.

Bullet got worked up whenever he thought about that night and how it played out; he felt like Jeffrey left him in the fire instead of sticking it out. He was also aware that no one was arrested for those murders, and so, he knew that the youngster was out there somewhere in the streets. Therefore, he made it his business to search daily, as he yearned for revenge.

"I hope this bitch ass young nigga don't think that this shit is over," said Bullet, as he puffed.

"Big homie, it's a small world. We'll catch him," said one of his shooters from the back seat.

"Facts!" Bullet nodded. "Oh, make sure that whoever sees him first, bring him to me. I wanna kill him myself," he commanded.

"No doubt," his soldiers replied.

For Bullet Head, this one was personal because he gave the

youngster a fair warning to not violate him or else there would be repercussions. However, that was precisely what Jeffrey did, he forgot all about the deal they made, and he did not keep his end of the bargain. After all, he just wanted revenge for his mother. He certainly did not want to get deeper into a life of crime and violence. Little did he know, he was dealing with a guy who neither forgives nor forgets. Now, Bullet was the one who was seeking revenge.

Chapter 12

For the first time in a long time, Jeffrey Jacob, who was 19 years old, had his life in proper order. After a couple of months of working with Bob, he moved into his own apartment, making him feel truly independent. He lived in Cordoba Courts apartment buildings, off 22nd Avenue, known in the streets as The Bricks. The rent for his one-bedroom apartment was $750 a month, but all his expenses were covered after only two weeks of work; then, the rest of his money he saved. He changed his mindset, thinking he had nothing to lose and nothing to live for, which often led to reckless actions. And instead, he placed more value on his life, abandoning all excuses while fighting for a better future. For the first time since his mother died, he was stable mentally, physically, spiritually, and financially. After being in the kitchen for so long with a master chef like Bobby King, he even developed some cooking skills. He had always been a fast learner, and he and Bob made a good team; they were building a bond that was not easy to rip asunder. Recently, Bob gave him a generous raise, and now, he was making well over 3 grand a month. His next move was to buy himself a car, which he was not far from doing since he had already put the word out. He started to furnish the place by purchasing a bed set and a sectional couch for the living room. The apartment came with certain appliances, like a refrigerator, a stove, and a microwave. Therefore, only a few things left that he needed, like TVs, a laptop, and some simple decorations.

Nevertheless, he was grateful for a place to call home, where he was comfortable and could get peace of mind. He practiced the cleanliness that his mother instilled in him, and he applied his new cooking skills in his personal kitchen. He purchased a new Samsung Galaxy cellular phone, and he also kept his wardrobe up to date, with presentable attire.

After all, he realized that his childhood days were long gone and that his parents were never coming back. Therefore, he woke up and smelled the coffee, faced his reality, and took on the challenges and the endeavors of being an adult. He was still young and had his whole life ahead of him. Therefore, he focused his attention on making progress. Moreover, he was grateful for the people present in his life, like Bobby King and his late father's right-hand man, who kept him close. Ever since they reunited, Og Boe picked him up almost every weekend, and they went out somewhere to have fun. He never had to spend a dollar whenever he was with Boe. In fact, he was impressed with the connections that the Og had in Miami. For instance, Boe knew most of the club owners, and wherever they went, they got in with no hassle and were treated special. Thanks to Boe, there was hardly a club in Miami that Jeffrey had not been to.

One Sunday morning, his cellphone rang, and it was Boe telling him to get dressed, that they were going to look at a car that one of his partners was selling. They already had discussed a price range of two to three thousand, so when Jeffrey got the call, he knew that things were looking good. He went to his stash and got the $2,000 that he had accumulated. Then, he got dressed and waited, and within the next thirty minutes, Og Boe pulled up. They went to check out the vehicle, a 2002 Honda Accord, dark grey with light tints, in well-maintained condition. It only had a little over 60,000 miles, and Jeffrey liked what he saw, but the man wanted $3,500 for it. Boe was a good negotiator, and he talked his partner down to $3,000 for right-away cash-out. The man accepted the offer, and Boe covered the thousand dollars that Jeffrey was missing, then they cashed out for the vehicle right then and there. Jeffrey was even more excited when he received the keys and the title; it was his first car, and he loved it.

"Big homie, I will pay you back as soon as possible," said Jeffrey to Og Boe before they departed.

"Don't even worry about it," Boe replied. "It's the least I can do."

Furthermore, Little Jeff was head over heels as he drove home in his new Honda Accord. Everything he desired was now in place, a good job, a nice house, and a reliable vehicle. Og Boe was like his uncle, and Bobby King was like his father; he held the utmost respect for them. Never failing to listen carefully to Bob's lectures, until he grew to be humble and patient, not indulging in too much excitement, but rather reserved and observant. The journey from who he was to who he was becoming made him proud of himself. Jeffrey recognized that the circumstances that he survived contributed a great deal to his growth.

A week later, he woke up one morning and said his prayers, and then, he thought about ordering breakfast for takeout. He was indecisive about what he wanted to eat, but he was sure about not cooking breakfast that morning, as he continued to enjoy the privileges of being mobile. Therefore, he grabbed his wallet from the nightstand to fetch his debit card and to check for any restaurant business cards that he might have had. However, as he went through his wallet, one of the first cards he came out with was a Wells Fargo bank business card, and the name on it read: Jane Walker. Then, suddenly her image appeared in his mind as he reminisced. He was tempted to give her a call, but he was hesitant. He contemplated because it had been over three months since they met, and he had not followed up with her since. He thought that she might have forgotten about him, and despite the apparent chemistry they shared, sometimes being out of sight is being out of mind. Jeffrey himself was so consumed with his situation that his focus had been solely on making progress.

Nevertheless, now that things were going smoothly in his life, he thought it would be nice to have a girl around, and Jane was the ideal candidate. Even though it had been years since he entertained a female, he had never lost his confidence. Therefore, he conquered his timidness, grabbed his phone, and dialed the mobile number on the card. He was still a little nervous as it rang, but someone answered after two rings, to his surprise.

"Hello, good morning. This is Jane," said a soft voice on the other end.

"Hi, Jane, good morning. This is Jeffrey. We met at the bank where you work a while back. Do you remember me?" he asked with a smile.

She was quiet for a moment. "I'm not sure if I do. You said that your name was Jeffrey?" she asked.

"Yes, that's right, Jeffrey, as in Jeffrey Jacob! You were supposed to be my personal banker. It was a couple months ago, but I never forgot about you," he replied.

When he said his full name, it rang a bell in Jane's head, and she smiled as she remembered. "As a matter of fact, I think I do remember you! Wasn't it back in January when you came to open your checking account?"

"That's correct! I'm glad you remember because you've been on my mind since I met you," said Jeffrey.

"Really? Well, that is hard to tell since it took you this long to call," she replied.

Jeffrey smiled. "I've just been really busy, putting some things in order, if you know what I mean."

"Yeah, I know how that goes," said Jane.

"So, how have you been?" Jeffrey asked.

"I have been great! You know, school and work. I'm actually at school right now, and my next class is about to start in a minute," she replied.

"That's excellent! Well, I would love to see you again. You should let me take you out to eat or something."

"Sure, I like to eat. How about lunch this afternoon?"

"Sounds like a plan! Just call me when you finish with your classes, and I'll take it from there."

"Ok, Jeff! Talk to you later," she replied, with a bit of excitement, and then she hung up.

"Yes!" Jeffrey yelled, and then he did his victory uppercut.

It was official, he had a pending date with the girl of his dreams, and he could not wait to see her. He canceled his plans for ordering breakfast and started preparing himself for his lunch date. Jane had been expecting him to call much sooner because she was attracted to his energy, and she wanted to get to know him better. Fortunately, the feeling was mutual, and Jeffrey did not have to try too hard to impress her. However, he picked out something nice to wear and checked to ensure that everything else was on point, seeing to it that he was well-groomed and that his car was clean. His plan was to take her to one of his favorite restaurants, Jackson's Soul Food, in Overtown. He had been there a few times with Og Boe and rated it as one of Miami's best breakfast and lunch spots.

He took a shower, and then he got dressed in a fitted white V-neck Polo T-shirt, some grey sweatpants, and a pair of white Air-Force1 sneakers. Two hours went by as if they were thirty minutes, and then, he received the call that he was expecting.

"Hey Jeff, my classes are over for today," said Jane. "Where are we meeting?"

"Okay. I will text you the address to the restaurant, and you can meet me there," Jeffrey replied.

When they got off the phone, he double-checked to make sure that he was not leaving anything, and then he got in his car and made his way to Overtown. As he drove south on I-95, he let all the windows down to feel the natural breeze, and it felt amazing. There wasn't much traffic on the road, so he made it to the restaurant in about 15 minutes, and then he texted her to let her know that he had arrived. She said that she was less than five minutes away, and he replied, perfect. While he waited, he sprayed on some cologne and then rechecked himself in the mirror; he really wanted everything to go right. Minutes later, a sky-blue Toyota Camry pulled into the parking lot, and Jane Walker got out of it, looking adorable. She wore a nicely fitting, colorful dress, which stopped right above her knees, some comfy sandals, and a small handbag. She was glowing, and her attire was simple, but it was still elegant.

Jeffrey was on point as he got out of his car quickly to greet her. "Hello, beautiful, it's nice to see you again. You look amazing!"

Jane smiled. "Hi, Jeff! Thank you, you look nice yourself," she replied, and then she gave him a hug.

The smell of her perfume gave him the chills, and her skin was glistening. She was the definition of beauty. "The pleasure is mines! I'm glad you came," said Jeffrey.

"I am happy to be here," Jane replied, blushing and showing off her dimples.

"Wonderful! Well, let's go inside."

They walked across the street from the parking lot to the restaurant. Jeffrey was confident that she would love the food because he was never disappointed with Jackson's.

"Good afternoon, welcome in! You guys can sit anywhere that is empty," said the hostess to the couple when they walked into the restaurant.

"Okay, thank you!" Jeffrey replied, and then they chose a booth by the window.

When they sat down, they skimmed through the menu as Jeffrey showed her everything he recommended. He had already tried a few different dishes on his recent visits. He already knew what he wanted—grilled Snapper fish, peas and rice, and collard greens. Jane decided to try the smothered chicken with candy yams and collard greens.

"You made a good choice," said Jeffrey to his date as the waitress took their orders.

"I hope so," she replied.

Then, as they waited on their food, they took the opportunity to find out more about each other

"So, where are you from originally?" Jeffrey asked.

"Oh, I was born right here in Florida. My father is African American, and my mother is Dominican. What about you?" she asked.

"I was born and raised in New Orleans," Jeffrey replied. "My mother and I moved here to Miami just a few years ago."

The date was rolling smoothly, and there wasn't a single dull moment as they got to know each other better. Jeffrey kept her entertained by being charming and making her laugh from time to time. He spoke about his hometown and compared it with Miami, pointing out the similarities and the many differences. Jane was tuned in because she knew nothing about New Orleans, and she wanted to know what it was like growing up there. She spoke about college and her goal to become an official banker; it was clear that she was dedicated to her studies and career. Jeffrey was impressed with her ambition and her dedication; she had beauty and brains.

The food arrived, and steam rose from the plates as the smell of the seasonings contacted their noses. They got right to it, and like always, the food was delicious. Jane was impressed and stated that Jackson's was going to be her new spot. The chemistry and the bond between them grew stronger as they continued to converse. Jeffrey was supportive and affectionate, which were the exact qualities that Jane looked for in a man. They ate until they were full, and then they wrapped up their lunch date. Jeffrey took care of the bill and left a nice tip for the waitress, and then they left. The date was perfect. They walked out of the restaurant hand in hand, knowing that more days like that were ahead of them.

Chapter 13

A few days later, Jeffrey and Bob were at the restaurant. The afternoon traffic was lighter than usual, so Bob asked Jeffrey to run a quick errand. He wanted Jeffrey to go and send money through Western Union to one of his relatives. Jeffrey, who would do anything for the elder, was glad to go. Therefore, he went and sent the money and returned to the restaurant within an hour. However, as he pulled back into the restaurant's parking lot, he noticed an altercation out front. To his surprise, the old man was involved in the conflict, and he was pretty worked up from the look of things. Jeffrey parked, and then he sat there for a minute to observe. He saw Ziona's car in the parking lot, and he figured that she must have gotten there not too long ago. Apparently, something went wrong while he was gone, which triggered the altercation, and he was trying to piece it together. The old man was arguing with a local gangster, who was shirtless, with his pants sagging down to his knees. Jeffrey was curious, so he got out of the car and went to see what was happening. As he drew closer, he overheard Bob giving the hoodlum a fair warning.

"I won't tell you anymore, to leave and don't come back here," Bob yelled.

"You don't know who you fucking with, old man!" The guy replied arrogantly.

Jeffrey, who had almost reached where they were standing, was going to see if he could do anything to resolve the issue.

However, Bob went on bitterly. "First, you disrespect my wife, and then when I said something about it, you act like you don't give a damn! So, you and your partner need to leave the premises immediately."

"Listen, man, fuck all that! I fucks with, who I wants to fuck with," said the hoodlum.

Then, before Jeffrey was close enough to prevent it, Bob landed a slap in the guy's face that sent him staggering. There were two of them, and the other one was walking out of the restaurant, just in time to catch his partner's reaction to the impact. Unfortunately, Jeffrey was distracted by the conflict. He and the other guy bumped right into each other, a collision so hard that it knocked them both off track.

"Nigga, watch where the fuck you going!" The guy yelled as Jeffrey gazed at him, puzzled.

Then, the one who was slapped interrupted them. "Don't sweat it, homie. Let's slide. They done fucked all the way up. We'll be back!" His partner bit his lip and nodded as he backed away. They mugged Jeffrey and Bob all the way back to their vehicle, and then they hopped in and peeled off, rushing out of the parking lot.

"Hey, Bob, you alright? What happened?" Jeffrey asked. He was clueless, and he needed some answers because he had never seen the elder in such a state.

"Jeff, things are out of order right now. I'm going to close early today. Just take the rest of the day off, and I will call you later so that we can meet up and talk," said Bob with melancholy. He was a bit vulnerable and distraught because those type of circumstances was what he always dreaded.

Jeffrey understood, and he replied. "No problem, King, take your time. I will be on standby waiting for your call."

It was clear to see that Bob needed time to clear his head, so Jeffrey walked back to his car, got in it, and drove off. He decided to head back home to relax and wait on Bob's call. As he drove home, his mind began to wander, and he thought about how suddenly things could change. Then, right when he was about to turn into his apartment buildings, his phone rang, and it was a call from Og Boe, so he answered.

"Lil Jeff, what's popping?" Boe asked, with excitement in his voice.

Jeffrey replied. "Nothing much, Big Homie, just pulling up to the crib."

"Ok, listen, swing by my apartment right now if you can. I have someone here that I want you to meet," said Boe abruptly.

"Absolutely! I'll be there in about ten minutes," Jeffrey replied.

"Ok, perfect!"

Jeffrey made a U-turn and went towards Liberty City to Boe's apartment; he was anxious to see who the Og wanted him to meet. He pulled up to the buildings and walked up the stairs to the second floor, straight to Boe's apartment. He knocked on the door, and it was opened immediately.

Og Boe greeted him with a handshake. "Right on! Jeffrey Jeff!"

"Waddup, big homie?" Jeffrey asked as he shook his hand.

When he walked in and closed the door, he saw a man in the living room sitting on the couch. The man looked like he was a little older than Boe, and his fashion style was rather unusual. He wore a short-sleeve button-up shirt, dress pants, and dress shoes, with a Kangol hat.

"Meet, Cedric Williams! He is the chairman of Prime-Time Promotions. Me and this fellow go way back," said Boe, and then they both giggled at what seemed to be an inside joke.

Jeffrey went over and shook the man's hand. "Nice to meet you, Mr. Williams."

"It's nice to meet you too, youngblood. Call me Cedric," the man replied, and then he continued. "So, I heard you got talent!"

Jeffrey smiled. "Yes, sir! I do have a special way with words."

The vibes at Boe's apartment were the total opposite of what he had just left at the restaurant.

"That's solid! What is your stage name?" Cedric asked.

"It's Kreation, with a K!" Jeffrey replied.

"I like that," said Cedric. "Listen, you might not know who I am, but I'm into the entertainment business. In fact, my company oversees most of the major events here in Miami and nationwide."

"Yeah, this man is official," Boe confirmed. "Lil Jeff, didn't I tell you that I got you?"

Jeffrey smiled. "You ain't never let me down," he replied. "Hey Cedric, again, it's a pleasure!"

Og Boe's network was quite impressive, and for Jeffrey, this connection was special. He was astonished because he saw his opportunity unfolding before his eyes, and he was ready to grab hold of it.

"Man, I can get you on stage easily," Cedric Williams went on, "in front of thousands of people. As a matter of fact, one of our biggest annual events is coming up in December. It is called the Miami Apollo. That would be the perfect platform to showcase your talent, and it gives you some time to prepare."

"Man, that's a blessing! I'm with it all the way," Jeffrey replied excitingly.

"Well, cool then. I'm looking forward to seeing you do your thing," said Cedric.

"Oh, you best believe it! Thank you, man I appreciate it," Jeffrey replied.

"Nephew, there you go! It's prime time, time to shine," Boe teased, and they all laughed.

Then, Cedric handed Jeffrey a flyer for the upcoming event, and it was looking glamorous. The show was to be held on the 5th of

December, in downtown Miami. Jeffrey was flattered, and he smiled when he thought about the famous quote, that it is not about what you know, but who you know. He was feeling much better than when he arrived at Boe's apartment, confused about the situation at the restaurant. Now, he was ready to go home and soak everything up, and therefore, he said his goodbyes.

"I appreciate you, Og. That was clutch! I'm about to make a run. I'll catch up with you later," said Jeffrey, and then he hugged Og Boe.

"You already know Lil Jeff, anytime," Boe replied.

"Cedric, thanks again, brother! I'll definitely be in touch," said Jeffrey, as he gave Cedric a handshake.

"No doubt, youngblood! Be safe," Cedric replied.

"Peace out, Lil Jeff," said Boe as Jeffrey made his way out the door.

"Peace," said Jeffrey.

He reflected on everything and thought about how perfect the timing could sometimes be. If the incident at the restaurant did not occur, he would still be at work, and most likely, unavailable for that meeting. However, it seemed like things were working in his favor; he made it home and went straight into the shower. After that, he lit some incense and rolled a joint; then, he sat in his living room and puffed it slowly.

He took some time to brainstorm. He analyzed the depths of emotions, realizing that he was in no position to judge Bob for his reactions to the conflict. He was just hoping that the old man was alright and that the situation would not escalate further. Moreover, now that he met Cedric Williams, he decided to focus more on his craft, which meant writing and reciting more often. He knew that he had the opportunity of a lifetime, and he did not plan on being shy about it.

Jeffrey sat there in his living room for a few hours until he dozed off. Around 7 p.m., he was awakened by the ring of his cellphone, and it was Bob who was finally calling.

"Hey Jeff, if you're not busy, come on over to the house so we can reason," said Bob.

"Sure, Bob. I will be there in about thirty minutes." Jeffrey replied.

Bob lived in North Miami on the east side of Opa Locka and the I-95, roughly a 20-minute drive from where Jeffrey was. Therefore, he left his apartment immediately and went straight to the Kings' family house.

When he arrived at Bob's house, he rang the doorbell, and Bob greeted him at the front door.

"Hey Jeff, good to see you," said Bob, and they shook hands.

"Hey, Bob, good evening," Jeffrey replied as he walked in. Then, he saw Ziona in the kitchen, and he waved to her. "Good evening, Ziona!"

"Hi Jeff, good evening! Make yourself at home," she replied.

Only Bob and his wife were there; the house was quiet and peaceful. Bobby led Jeffrey to the garage, where his man cave was set up. He had a couch in there, a TV, and a bookstand with many books. When they sat down, Jeffrey handed him the receipt from the Western Union transaction

"I took care of the transaction for you earlier," said Jeffrey.

"Alright, thank you, Jeff!" Bob replied.

Then, Ziona walked in with a tray like a waitress with appetizers for them both. "Here is some fresh-squeezed lemonade and a few slices of carrot cake that I baked myself," she announced with a smile.

"Thank you, honey," said Bob.

"This is right on time, Ms. Ziona," Jeffrey added.

"No problem, enjoy," she replied and then left them to converse.

Ziona was Bob's backbone and his everything. She contributed much to their progress and well-being. Furthermore, as they munched,

Bob began to tell Jeffrey about what had happened earlier when he left to run the errand.

It all started about 15 minutes before Jeffrey returned when the two hoodlums walked into the restaurant. One of them had no shirt on, which was already a violation of the rules, but they were only buying juices, so to keep the peace, Bob decided to serve them quickly. However, about five minutes later, when the hoodlums were about to walk out, Ziona came in. That is when all hell broke loose.

The one with no shirt on took a shot immediately. "God damn, baby! You're fine as hell," he exclaimed as he looked her up and down.

Ziona was disturbed. "Excuse me?" she replied.

His partner laughed. "Nigga, you're crazy as hell! I'm 'bout to take a leak right quick," he yelled and went towards the bathroom.

The shirtless gangster continued. "You heard me, baby, you're fine as hell. I need you in my life!"

Now, Bob, who overheard the conversation, yelled from behind the counter. "Hey, man, show some respect! That is my wife you are talking to."

For some reason, the guy took him for a joke, and he laughed. "Nice try, old man, but you wouldn't know what to do with all this," he replied.

Ziona, who did not expect such behavior from anyone, was now truly upset. "Young man, you need to watch your mouth and show some respect," she warned him.

"Come on, baby, you need a real nigga in your life," the hoodlum beckoned, and then, he tried to grab her hand.

That was where he crossed the line, and Ziona slapped his hand away. "Boy, don't fool yourself," she yelled.

At that point, Bob had seen and heard enough, and he came from behind the counter with force. Without saying another word, he pushed the guy so hard that he went flying. Then, Bob grabbed him and shoved him outside. It was a little after this when Jeffrey pulled into the parking lot and saw the altercation. The guy he bumped into was the one who had gone to the bathroom and was just walking outside.

After hearing the whole story, everything made more sense, and Jeffrey understood why Bob reacted the way he did. However, deep down, Bob was still troubled and quite displeased with the outcome of the situation.

He stated. "See, Jeff, what happened earlier was no coincidence. Those guys were looking for trouble, and they had it coming."

"No doubt, Bob. That was straight disrespect!" Jeffrey replied.

"I don't know what the world has come to. These days people have no morals or decency," said Bob as he shook his head.

"I agree," said Jeffrey. "Why can't we all have unity? Why can't we all just be free?" he asked.

"Well, we must first free our minds. Many people are caught up in the matrix, in the great illusion. But, no matter how bad things look, the Almighty is always in control," said Bob, as the conversation geared towards some general topics.

Jeffrey nodded. "Now, let me ask you a question that has been on my mind for a while. How do we know which one is the true religion?" he asked.

Bob was quiet for a minute, and then he began. "Listen, son, there is something more important than any religion, and that is to have a real relationship with the Creator. Whether you are a Jew, a Muslim, or a Christian, we are all held responsible for our decisions and actions. Life is an opportunity to live and to love," said Bob sincerely.

"Basically, we should just live and let live," Jeffrey confirmed.

"Exactly! Life is too short for hatred and grudge," Bob added.

They allowed their minds to reach higher heights with sound reasoning as they touched on relevant topics. Jeffrey was gaining clarity and increasing his knowledge as he spoke with the wise man.

"Hey, Bob, how do you know when the time is right for something, like the moment of your destiny?" he asked.

Bob smiled. "Mr. Jacob, just like the mighty sun upon the horizon at the crack of dawn, so will you know when it is your time to shine," he replied.

Jeffrey nodded. "Yes, sir!"

The old man shared some of his purest thoughts, and most of Jeffrey's questions were answered. In a timely fashion, the reasoning was a relief for them both.

Chapter 14

The next day, the restaurant was open at its regular hours, and for the entire day, everything went smoothly. Then, three more days passed, and still, there was no follow-up from the incident. Those days had been gloomy because no one knew what to expect, and there was a bit of paranoia in the air. Bob had not been the same since the incident occurred. It was as if those gangsters struck the wrong nerves making him even more reserved. Jeffrey was just going along with the flow, being a strength to the operation when it was needed most. He got deeper into poetry, writing, and reciting some of his deepest thoughts during most of his alone time. The rest of his time he spent on the phone talking to Jane. Her soft voice was like ice water on a sunny afternoon. They got well acquainted and much closer until their relationship became official.

Jane was 21 years old, working towards her master's degree in college and majoring in Finance. She was multilingual, Spanish was her second language, and she spoke it fluently thanks to her mother. Her life rotated around school, work, and home, leaving little to no time for idling. She lived downtown in a luxurious two-bedroom condo that her parents bought for her. Harvey Walker was a real estate broker, and his business was doing very well; he gave his daughter full support.

Many years ago, her young and beautiful mother, Pricilla, migrated to Miami from the Dominican Republic. Mr. Harvey fell in love the day he met her, and in less than a year, they were happily married. They went on to have two children, first Harvey Jr. Walker and then Jane Walker. Harvey Jr. was already working in the real estate business; he was an agent in their father's brokerage. However, Jane had no interest in buying and selling properties; she wanted to do something different, so she chose banking. She was coming from good roots. It made her ambitious; her priorities were in order, and she was entirely focused. Jeffrey had no doubt that she would have loved Jane as her daughter-in-law if his mother was alive.

Furthermore, they knew each other's schedules from top to bottom, and they would be on the phone during her lunch breaks or between classes. Jeffrey was the spark that Jane needed; she loved his personality. She felt comfortable talking to him about anything because he was a good listener. He was also a natural charmer who made her laugh without even trying. Besides that, they really inspired each other.

One Wednesday afternoon, while Jeffrey was on break at work, he received a call from Jane. "Hey honey, how are you?" she asked.

"I'm good, sweetheart," Jeffrey replied. "What you got going on?"

"I'm cooking," said Jane. "Would you like to come over for dinner after work?"

"Yes, ma'am! That sounds like a plan," Jeffrey exclaimed. He was glad for the invite because it would be his first time going to her place, and it was an opportunity to be one-on-one with the girl of his dreams.

Furthermore, for the rest of the time at work, he anticipated the dinner date; and when he left, he went straight home to freshen up. She had already given him the directions to get to her condo, so he made his way to downtown Miami after he got dressed. She lived in the Epic Residences building, off Biscayne boulevard; it was a new development, and it was spectacular. He made it there in less than an hour, and then he went up to the 25th floor of the high-rise building where her condo was located. He knocked on the door, and when she opened it, they hugged and kissed right there at the doorway.

"Hey, honey, come on in," said Jane.

"Damn, it smells good in here!" Jeffrey exclaimed when he walked in.

Jane laughed. "Thank you," she replied.

The décor of her condo was like an art gallery: picture frames and paintings, modern style furniture, and mounted flat-screen TVs. The dinner table was set, with knives and forks, wine glasses, and a bottle of red wine. Slow jams came from a surround sound at a decent volume, and the atmosphere was nice and cozy.

"Your house is very nice," said Jeffrey as he looked around.

"Thank you," she replied. "Wait till you see the view from the balcony!"

The lights were dimmed, candles were burning, and the mood was set for relaxation. Jeffrey wanted to stay there forever. His girl was lightly dressed in thin silk shorts and a blouse with a colorful design, complimenting her figure every time she moved. The dinner was ready. She had made oxtails, peas and rice, cabbage, and potato salad. Jeffrey was impressed as he observed her cooking skills; he assisted her in taking the plates to the table, as he admired the romantic setting.

"Sweetheart, this looks delicious," said Jeffrey as they sat down.

"Let's just say that I know my way around the kitchen," she replied, and they laughed.

Then, when they were seated, they said a prayer together, and then Jeffrey popped open the bottle of wine. He filled the glasses, then they began to eat. The food tasted as good as it looked and smelled, and Jeffrey was sold as he tried a little bit of everything.

"This is yummy! I'm impressed," said Jeffrey.

Jane smiled. "I'm glad you like it!"

"Absolutely! So, how was your day?" he asked as they continued to eat.

"Oh, it was great! Work was busy, so the day went by fast," she replied. "How was yours?"

"Mine was cool, but this is the best part so far."

The dinner was hitting the spot, and the red wine was there to top it off; they were both feeling carefree as they filled their stomachs. Then, when they were done eating, he helped her clear the table, and she placed the dishes into the dishwasher. Jane was the type to clean up while cooking, so the kitchen wasn't near messy.

"Thank you for dinner babes, you damn sure put your foot in that one!" Jeffrey mentioned as he watched her move around in the kitchen.

"You are very welcome, my dear," she replied, and then she turned off the lights when she was finished.

They were feeling good and tipsy from eating and drinking, and again, Jeffrey took the initiative to refill the glasses. He was convinced that Jane was wifey material, and he wanted her in his life in every way possible. She took him by the hand and led him to the balcony to show him the view. The minute he stepped out there, he was blown away; the view was amazing. They were 25 feet above the ground, looking over the city, at nightfall when it was most beautiful. The constellations and the moon lit the sky as the city lights lit the city below.

"I would like to propose a toast," said Jeffrey, as he raised his glass to the heavens. Jane followed suit and raised her glass, and then Jeffrey continued. "To us, and to happiness!"

"To us!" Jane replied.

They took a sip and felt the tingle, and then Jeffrey looked away into the far distance; he was feeling refreshed as his mind took him on a quick journey. He reflected briefly on his progress over the years, but still, he knew that the best was yet to come. That view was all the motivation he needed! And as he soaked up the moment, he returned his focus back to Jane, with much admiration; and he watched as her hair blew in the wind.

She looked into his eyes and said, "Jeffrey, I love you!"

He could not help but smile. "I love you too, sweetheart," he replied. It was the first time that they had exchanged those words, and it was genuine. He pulled a folded paper from out of his pocket, and then he continued. "I got something for you."

"Really? What is it?" she asked excitingly.

"It's a poem that I wrote for you," Jeffrey replied.

"That is so sweet! Come on, let me hear it," she insisted.

"It's called 'Black Love,'" he began.

"As I testify orally, your body speaks poetry,
supposedly, led to me, feet that have glided through heavenly
isles
from looking in your eyes to deep between your thighs,
then I lay, where beauty lies.
Our love is a reflection of God's love,
so we should make love, and then call it –
Black Love!"

His voice made love to her ears, and her body tingled as chills ran up her spine. She jumped into his arms when he was finished and yelled. "Oh my god, babes, I love it!"

Her fragrance made his passion grow, and he held her tightly as he took a minute to undress her with his eyes. Then, they shared a long, wet kiss, and romance was in the air. The chemistry between them was alive, and when Jane felt the wetness of her vagina, she motioned for him to head back inside. It was his lucky night, and he knew he had to go for a home run.

"You know, it has been a couple years since I been intimate with a guy," said Jane timidly as they walked inside.

Jeffrey replied. "Word?"

"Yeah," she continued. "I broke up with my high school boyfriend about a month after we graduated. I found out that he had gotten another girl pregnant, and it broke my heart. Since then, I've just been focused on me."

"Well, that's his loss. That guy is crazy stupid," said Jeffrey. He had not been well acquainted with any female, but he kept that to himself.

Jane led Jeffrey straight to her bedroom, which was luxurious with a king-size bed. Jeffrey was quick on his feet, and he held her hand and pulled her in closely; the thin material of her clothing allowed him to feel every curve of her body. He got rid of his shirt, and then he rubbed her down while sucking on her cherry lips. They kissed for a couple minutes, and then Jane took a step back. He watched her from the eye of the tiger as she began to undress. First, she took off her blouse and then the silky shorts until she was down to her bra and panties, and that is when she did a slow 360 spin. Jeffrey shook his head and licked his lips. His erection was evidence of his excitement. Then, Jane got rid of the last two pieces until she was completely naked, and indeed, she was a beautiful sight. She had the body of a goddess. Her breasts were firm and perky, her stomach was flat, and her legs were strong and sexy. To top it off, she had the prettiest pussy in the world, and her ass was fat, in the best way. He quickly got rid of his pants, and now, he was down to his socks and boxers. Then, without hesitation, he grabbed his queen and started feeling all over her body, kissing her neck and sucking on her nipples. His aggressiveness made her get even wetter, and he was as hard as a rock. Her nipples got stiff as the temperature rose. He lifted her up and lay her on the bed, and then he wet his fingers and began to play with her clitoris. She was wet and ready to feel him inside as she moaned with pleasure. Therefore, he dropped his boxers, and then he slowly entered the gates of paradise. Immediately, her muscles gripped his penis, and she cried as he pushed it further. It was time for him to go to work; her vagina was tight, but the soaking wetness made it easier to penetrate. He placed her legs on his shoulders and started digging in as if he had found a gold mine. She was pleased with how he was finding all the right spots, especially when he held her legs in his hands and spread them far apart. He was focused, and he increased the pace and the intensity until she screamed at the top of her lungs.

After a while, they went out to the living room and picked up where they had left off on the sofa. Jane called him Daddy as he drilled her from the side, putting down some of his best work ever. Her vagina was now loose, and her body was shaking as he struck deep; they were all over each other and all over the house. Love was in the making as she cried tears of joy, and Jeffrey continued to show off his stroke. He had a point to prove because he knew better than to blow his first chance with the girl of his dreams.

Furthermore, when he took her out to the balcony and bent her over, she was turned on by his boldness. The view was even more wonderful now from where he was standing, and he gripped her waistline and slid back into her guts, where it was warm and gushy. Then, he penetrated her steadily from the back as he stood firm, adding occasional roughness to his demeanor.

"Thank you, baby!" Jane cried, and her voice echoed in the night's air.

She threw her ass backward rapidly towards him. After a while, he had to pull out quickly to prolong the inevitable. However, it was not long before he went back in and reapplied the pressure, with a hard stabbing, stamina banging, incredible backshot. His rod was covered with her juices as she experienced multiple orgasms. Then, the next time he nearly reached his climax, he pulled out once again and took her back inside to finish off on the couch. She was dripping wet when she climbed on top and sat on his joystick, and then, she bounced up and down as he stood rock hard in her guts. The couch was rocking. It was a bumpy ride as he signed his name on her slippery walls. Then, once again, her walls came tumbling down.

"Daddy! I'm coming!" she screamed.

Up and down like a pogo stick, she continued to bounce, and then eventually, she came all over his dick. Her vagina pulsated while she twerked and made her ass clap, and that did it for Jeffrey, as he suddenly exploded. For some reason, he stayed in as his sperms shot up in her guts, and she sat there until he was finished. Seamen began to drip down her thighs, and they held each other and kissed. It felt like heaven on earth, and every second of it was marvelous; her postman was there, with a special delivery.

Chapter 15

Two days later, Friday morning around 11:30 a.m. Jeffrey's cellphone rang. It was Og Boe, so he answered.

"Lil Jeff, what's popping?" Boe asked.

"I'm cooling, Og! Here at work," Jeffrey replied.

"Ok, cool. I'm coming there for lunch today, in about an hour or so. You know I fucks with the vegetarian vibe from time to time," said Boe.

Jeffrey laughed. "No problem, big homie. I'll see you when you get here."

"Ok then. One!"

It had only been thirty minutes since the restaurant was open to the public. There were already two customers in the lobby. Jeffrey and Bob were there since 10 a.m., preparing for what was usually one of the busiest days of the week. Almost all the morning's work was in the kitchen, with prepping and cooking the meal of the day. If the food ran low during the day, which it often did, Bob would start cooking another batch before it ran out. Instead of cooking too much at one time, he chose to do that to keep everything fresh. So far, the morning was off to a good start, as Jeffrey left the kitchen to assist the customers who were in the lobby.

Unfortunately, it was not a good morning over on Ali Baba Avenue, as Bullet Head and his crew were busy loading their clips with ammunition. Word got back to Bullet that Jeffrey was working at

Bobby's Meals, and now the Opa Locka's drug lord was ready to pay the young man a visit.

The incident that happened at the restaurant last week, when the hoodlums disrespected Bob and his wife, was a terrible coincidence. Those guys were two of Bullet's main soldiers. That day, they were out and about, up to no good. The one Bob had slapped was Trevor; he was a maniac. The other one who Jeffrey bumped into was Block, a cold-blooded murderer who was one of Bullet's top shooters. When they knocked each other off track, Block recognized Jeffrey from the description that Bullet gave, and that was why he was mugging and staring so hard. However, he remembered that Bullet specified that he wanted to kill the youngster himself, which was the only reason why Block did not lash out.

Flashback to when the hoodlums peeled off and rushed out of the restaurant's parking lot. Within the next ten minutes, they pulled up on Bullet.

"Bossman, you won't believe who we just ran into," said Block with a rush of adrenaline.

"Who?" Bullet asked inquisitively.

"Your boy, Jeffrey. He was at Bobby's, that vegetarian restaurant down the street. I think he work there," said Block.

"Say what?" Bullet exclaimed. "I knew that lil nigga day was gonna come!" He was excited about the long-sought discovery.

"Yeah, and that old man who run the place had the nerves to slap me. We need to go handle that shit right now," said Trevor angrily.

However, Bullet disagreed. "Nah, let's give it about a week to let the tension die down, and then we will give them motha fuckas everything we got."

"Ok, main man, say less," Trevor replied, and then they all nodded in agreement.

Inevitably, the wait was over, and it was time to make a move;

that Friday was judgment day.

"We finna smash that motha fucka, and everything else in that bitch, ya heard me!" Bullet exclaimed as he puffed marijuana smoke and drove the T-bird to yet another bloody mission.

Block agreed. "You damn right! I ain't sparing nothing!"

They were three men deep with heavy artillery. The man in the back seat was Trevor, who had disrespected Ziona; he was armed with a 50 clip AK-47 rifle, also known as the Choppa. Bullet and Block were in the front, and they were both carrying their favorite tools, twin Glocks with 32 round extension clips. The crew's plan was to go in and shoot up the restaurant and kill everyone in there, and they were going to execute in broad daylight, with no questions asked.

Back over at Bobby's Meals, so far, it had been a quiet, peaceful day. The loudest noise was coming from the television in the lobby. Bobby and Jeffrey were in the kitchen when they heard the doorbell, which meant that someone had walked in. Therefore, Jeffrey went to check it out.

"Bles-sed love! Selassie lives," said the Rastaman who came in. "One large, please!"

"Bles-sed love! One large, coming up," Jeffrey replied, and then he went to the kitchen to prepare the man's order.

At 12:45 in the afternoon, Bullet and his gang pulled into the Bobby's Meals parking lot. They jumped out of the Thunderbird with their hoodies on and their weapons in hand, ready to regulate. Bobby, Jeffrey, and the Rastaman were the only ones in there when the killers walked in. Immediately, the gunmen began to operate like the special forces. Bullet made his way toward the front counter, and Trevor followed him with the rifle while Block stayed back to keep an eye on the door. The Rastaman was in shock when he saw what was about to unfold, and so was Jeffrey, who was just coming back from the kitchen with the large plate. He noticed the intruders, and he recognized Bullet when they made eye contact, and that was when he knew that it was over. His facial expression was as if he had seen a ghost, especially when Bullet lifted the two Glocks and pointed them in his direction. Jeffrey wanted to disappear, but he had no superpowers, and the next thing you know, Bullet began to let it ring. Spent shells hit the ground while 40 caliber bullets went rapidly towards Little Jeff. He tried to escape but was unfortunately hit by a couple blows. The impact was so crucial that the plate fell from his hands and splattered on the ground as he collapsed, and everything went blank.

The Rastaman yelled. "Bumbo-Clawt!"

Then, Trevor decided to put the AK 47 to use, activating his trigger finger while swinging the rifle from side to side; bullets went everywhere and destroyed everything. Bullet Head got out of the way quickly, but the Rastaman was not so lucky, as several gunshots ripped through his chest and caused him to tumble over. His body slumped on the ground, and his blood splashed on the walls; the scene was already messy. As the Choppa continued to rip, the showcase counter shattered and broke, while picture frames and banners fell from their high places.

Momentarily, the three killers drew closer to what was left of the counter, and they peeped over to make sure that the target was dead. However, when they looked, they saw no one; Jeffrey was somehow gone. The murderers, who were expecting to see a dead body, exchanged a strange look amongst themselves. Then, Bullet noticed the blood trail, and he motioned his crew to head towards the kitchen. Indeed, it was Bobby King who acted quickly and made the courageous move. When he heard the first gunshots, he crouched towards the front and saw Jeffrey lying there wounded. Therefore, while the rifle was going off, he pulled the lad back into the kitchen, where he did everything in his power to seize the blood flow.

As the killers moved towards the kitchen, a barrage of gunshots came rapidly from behind them. Og Boe came to buy lunch as he promised but realized upon arrival that there was an issue. Good thing, Boe was the type to react quickly, save all his questions for later, and lead his way through the front door with gunshots from his Desert Eagle.

He caught the intruders with their backs turned, and he exercised his years of experience as he allowed his pistol to bark loudly. By the time Bullet Head tried to turn around and look, he was the first to get caught with a head shot, and he fell instantly, face-first to the ground. Trevor was also hit one time in his upper body, but he was still standing. So, he turned the Choppa in Boe's direction and squeezed aggressively on the trigger. Fortunately, Boe was skillful with such matters, and he dove quickly, firing as he landed. Two to three more bullets flew through the rifle man's stomach and chest, and he lost his footing. A few more wild shots were fired from the AK 47 as he went down, only to add more damage to the restaurant. Block, who had found cover, was full of rage; so, he emptied his clips in the area where Boe landed. Og Boe tried to maneuver; however, he was hit multiple times from the many rounds that came towards him, and he crashed.

Block was the last man standing, and while blood continued to gush from the dead bodies, he grabbed the Choppa off the ground and made his way towards the front door. Nevertheless, the police were just rushing into the parking lot, slamming on their brakes, positioning themselves. Therefore, Block made it outside, only to be surrounded by many officers ready to apprehend him. He was armed and dangerous and ready to shoot when he realized that there was no escape. Every cop who was on the scene had their aim locked in on the target.

"Drop your weapon!" One of the officers yelled on the PA system.

Block mumbled. "Oh shit!"

However, he chose death over life in prison. Therefore, seconds later, he tried to finish the clip of the assault rifle.

"Fuck off, you pigs!" he yelled as he squeezed the trigger and waved the rifle around like a madman.

Gunshots ricocheted off the squad cars, and some of the cops scrambled to find cover. However, they immediately returned fire, and hundreds of rounds from different weapons, including fully automatics, swarmed Block like bees in a hive. Bullet wounds filled his body with holes like a strainer, and the impact lifted him off his feet and threw him asunder; he was ripped apart and dead before he landed on the ground. Finally, the madness ended, and the cops rushed into the restaurant. Only to find dead bodies on the ground and gun smoke still in the air. It was a blood bath, bullet holes were everywhere, and everything was destroyed. Ambulances were en route while the crime scene unit swarmed the building, took pictures, and made notes, attempting to identify the bodies.

On the floor in the kitchen, Jeffrey lay in critical condition, but he was still breathing. Bobby King was the only one who did not get shot, and he was there doing everything he could to stop Jeffrey from bleeding out. When Jeffrey made eye contact with Bullet Head, his adrenaline rushed, and he tried to turn around and run back into the kitchen. Unfortunately, Bullet's reflex was too quick, and when he squeezed, Jeffrey was caught twice, one time in his shoulder and once in his ribcage. It was a pitiful sight to see the old man there on the floor, covered in Jeffrey's blood and filled with sorrow. Even though he was unharmed physically; mentally, he was traumatized.

The paramedics arrived, and they rushed into the restaurant's kitchen after being told that there were survivors. They went through their procedures quickly, checking to ensure there was still a pulse. Then they carried the wounded lad away to the ambulance. Bob saw the desolation of his business, the years of hard work that he dedicated demolished, and it crushed his heart. Nevertheless, he refused to leave Jeffrey's side, so he rode to the hospital with him in the ambulance. Jeffrey was hooked up to a ventilator, and the paramedics found ways to block the wounds and stop the blood from flowing. The ambulance rushed out of the parking lot, which was then overcrowded with cars and people, unlike two hours earlier, when it was nearly empty.

It had been a massacre in broad daylight, and the murder scene was chaotic as noise filled the air. Crowds of people came from left and right to spectate, but no one except the crime scene unit was allowed access to the restaurant. Everything was dark and silent in Jeffrey's head as he traveled to the emergency room, and he felt like he was being transcended to another realm.

The crime scene unit announced the body count back at the restaurant, five in total, and then they began hauling out the body bags.

Miguel Bash

Chapter 16

The cycle of karma is never-ending, trapping men into its web, genuinely unpredictable one must be, for a chance to escape its course.

One month later, Jeffrey Jacob was still at Jackson North hospital, fighting desperately for his life. He was unresponsive when he first arrived at the emergency room. Therefore, he was taken straight to the Intensive Care Unit. From then, he was in a coma for roughly nine days. He was in a critical condition, barely hanging on to his life. The bullet to his shoulder went in and out, but the one that went through his ribcage was still in his body. By the grace of God, during his second week of being hospitalized, he started to show a little progress. Then, when the doctors were convinced that he was mentally and physically stable enough, they carried him into surgery to locate and remove the bullet that remained in his body. After general anesthesia, the surgeons performed hours of operation where they had to be precise and cautious. The shoulder wound took a chunk of his flesh, but with over thirty stitches, they closed it up as neatly as possible. The bullet that remained in his body was life-threatening, and they had to cut into his flesh to find and remove it. Thanks to the advancement of technology and the surgeons' expertise, they could locate the bullet, which had settled inches from his spinal cord. Some of his tissues were ripped apart, but fortunately, none of his major organs were damaged. If the bullet had touched his spine, he would have certainly been crippled and maybe even dead. However, the surgeons did a tremendous job, and the surgery ended up being frighteningly successful. Many people had lost hope, thinking that he would not make it out alive, but the ones who loved him most never stopped believing.

Jeffrey had to relearn everything that he once did easily and naturally. As time went by, he became more responsive, recognized the people in his room, and smiled whenever they were being humorous. He was profoundly grateful to have survived such injuries. The fact that he was still alive was his sole motivation for recovery. Also, he realized that he had a strong support system with the few people who had his best interest at heart. Bobby King and his family were there at the hospital, day in and night out, whenever time allowed, ensuring that the nurses were doing their job. His girlfriend, Jane, was also by his side, keeping hope alive and proving that she was loyal. When she first heard the news, which aired on television the same day that it happened, she was devastated. She stopped what she was doing immediately and rushed down to the hospital. She became well acquainted with Bob and his family since they were all there most of the time. They prayed together and stood together in faith, believing without a doubt that Jeffrey was going to pull through; the energy in the room was always positive. Nowadays, visiting the hospital had become a part of Jane's daily schedule; she would leave school and go straight to see Jeffrey unless she had to work. Then, she would visit him afterward. Ironically, the predicament brought them even closer together.

One day, when they were alone in the room, they engaged in a personal conversation.

"I love you, Jeff! And I know that it's not over. You will pull through this eventually," said Jane sincerely.

"Thank you, sweetheart! I love you too. And you really don't have to say anything because your actions speak for themselves," Jeffrey replied.

"Thank you, honey. Oh, and when you make it home, I have a wonderful surprise for you," said Jane.

"Really? Can you tell me now? Jeffrey asked.

"No, Jeff. We should wait," Jane replied, and they laughed.

After barely escaping death, Jeffrey had no doubt that he was still breathing for a special purpose. At times, he looked back at his life. He was humbled by his experiences because they made him stronger mentally and emotionally. As time went on, he got better physically. He talked and laughed more often, sometimes even walked around. His support system was hoping for a speedy recovery. However, when he heard that Boe was dead, it broke his heart and saddened his mood for a few days. Jeff knew that he would miss having the Og around; because that was the closest person to his dad, as far as personality, the overall New Orleans's style, and the TBG's flavor. To lose Og Boe was to lose someone who genuinely loved him, and in a world where not many people were genuine, you hate to lose the few you have.

Despite all the heartache and damage, every police officer in Miami had reasons to celebrate because some of the city's most wanted gangsters were now deceased. Bullet Head was the most notorious of them all, the police had been looking for him for years, but whenever they got close, he always found a way to slip out of their fingers. They still did not recognize Jeffrey from the night when he killed Beans because they never did get a clear view of his face. Therefore, it was just another unsolved murder, just like Ms. Elaine's case and many others; he was free from his past as far as Jeffrey was concerned.

Many numbers and signs appeared to him while he was hospitalized, which gave him hints of a new beginning. Then, he realized that he had to be delivered entirely from his past for him to really start new. He was grateful beyond words, and he owed it all to Bob; it was the second time the old man had saved his life. He felt like Bob deserved his honesty, and therefore, one day, when they were alone in the room, Jeffrey told him the truth.

"Hey, Bob, I thought you should know," Jeffrey began. "I made a deal with the guy who led me to my mother's killer. He wanted me to join his gang as a way to return the favor. I accepted the offer, even though I had no interest in becoming a gang member. However, it happened that we had to split up, and the agreement was breached. That is the same guy who came with his friends to shoot up the restaurant and kill everyone in it, just to seek revenge. I feel like the massacre was my fault, and I am sorry for leading such destruction into a peaceful atmosphere," said Jeffrey.

Bob was alarmed when he heard that information, but he also appreciated the young man's honesty. "Don't blame yourself for anything, Jeff. Right now, you should only focus on recovering. I understand that you were spiritually blind at the time when you were in the streets," Bob replied.

"I certainly was," said Jeffrey. "Now I realize that nothing good came from seeking revenge, only an ongoing cycle of bad karma."

Bobby King had reached the end of his journey in serving the public. After the rampage at the restaurant, he retired from the business. He was 81 years old, so he decided to dedicate the last years of his life to his family and relax. He finally had enough of the stress that came with running the business, and even worse, now to rebuild it. Therefore, Bobby's Meals was officially out of business, and it was a painful loss for the community. Many people were committed to the diet, and the restaurant played a significant role in their lives. However, Bob had served them faithfully for more than 30 years. He witnessed many changes over time, but he had never seen anything as ruthless as the massacre. Therefore, that was where he drew the line.

Jeffrey Jacob was still dealing with some inner conflicts personally. Sometimes, when he was alone, he would cry out loudly. Asking questions like: "Oh life, where is your preciousness?" "Why am I still alive?" And. "What is my purpose?"

He would often beat himself up with guilt, blaming himself for how things unfolded, causing the loss of innocent lives. It was difficult for him to grasp how he went so quickly from having everything he ever wanted to nearly lose it all. However, despite his insecurities, he continued to make progress towards recovery. The wounds were not completely healed, they were still tender, but he was strong enough to move around and help himself with certain things. There was an occasional pain in his ribs and abdominal area. Still, outwardly, he was looking fit enough that a stranger would have no clue that he had been shot twice. After looking so closely into the face of death, he placed a lot more emphasis on his life, increasing his level of patience and paying more attention to details. Even though he was not pleased with how it all ended, he was glad that the rivalry between him and Bullet was a thing of the past and that he no longer had to look over his shoulders. Nevertheless, he wasn't planning on taking the experience lightly nor his survival for granted. Those types of situations usually amounted to nothing. It was just another day in the ghetto, but this one was the gasoline that the fire inside of Jeffrey needed; it was reformation.

After a little over two months in the hospital, the doctors considered him strong enough to be discharged. They were amazed by the speed of his recovery from such injuries. It was a beautiful sunshiny day when he stepped outside of the hospital. He was greeted immediately by the smell of fresh air. Therefore, he took a minute to inhale and exhale it, and then, he and his girlfriend made their way over to the Kings' family house. Bobby and his family had put together a welcome home party for Jeffrey to lift his spirit from being bedridden for such a long time. It was a very thoughtful token of their love. After all, everyone wanted to see him shake back, and his return was long-awaited.

"My love, I want you to move in with me. That way, I can continue to assist you with whatever you need. At least, until you are fully recovered," said Jane convincingly as she drove.

"That sounds good to me, babe," Jeffrey replied. "I will just need to get a few things from my apartment."

Jane smiled. "Okay, great!"

When they arrived at the Kings' house, they received a warm welcome with much excitement; and it was precisely what Jeffrey needed, people, food, and music. He was never fond of the food in the hospital, so he ate like he was fresh off a two-month fast. He also drank some of the best homemade natural juices. Then, he danced and fellowshipped when his belly was full, expressing his gratitude, toasting to life. They celebrated at the King's house for a few hours until it got late, and then they prepared to leave. Ziona fixed a few plates for them to carry home while they said their goodbyes to everyone, and then, they made their way downtown to the condo. Jane maneuvered through the little traffic on the I-95 while Jeffrey put his seat back and relaxed. It was not long before they pulled into the garage of the Epic Residences building and then to the elevator.

As the elevator took them to the 25th floor, Jane began. "So, my love, are you ready for your wonderful surprise?" she asked.

"Oh yes," Jeffrey replied. "Never for a minute did I forget!"

They both smiled, and then when they made it inside the condo, she led him to the guest room and opened the door.

"Voila!" she exclaimed.

Jeffrey noticed that the room was redecorated. It was painted blue, with toys and a baby's crib. However, he was still a little slow to grasp what was really happening.

"Is this what I think it is?" he asked.

Jane smiled. "That's right, Jeff! I'm pregnant," she replied.

"Wow! My love, that is amazing," said Jeffrey, scrambling for words to express himself.

"I know, baby! I am 11 weeks right now. I didn't want to tell you until you got home," she replied.

"Well," said Jeffrey, "it is indeed a wonderful surprise!"

Jane was excited that she was having his baby. "Oh, it's a boy, I can feel it. I can't wait to confirm that at the ultrasound appointment."

Jeffrey was somewhat lost for words. He had no idea that she was pregnant, she did an excellent job keeping it a secret, and it was the last thing he was expecting to hear. It did not matter for him, whether it was going to be a boy or a girl, just the thought alone of bringing a child into the world gave him a lot to think about. He was not sure if he was ready for such a step, but whether he was or not, he was happy to be taking that step with Jane. One thing that he was sure about was that she was the one with whom he wanted to spend the rest of his life.

After soaking up the moment, they went into the master bedroom and showered together, and then, they went to bed. That night, of course, they made sweet love.

Chapter 17

Living in downtown Miami was the best life that Jeffrey lived since he and his mother migrated to South Florida. He could not get enough of waking up to Jane's natural beauty and then to the view that overlooks the city. It was an upper-echelon lifestyle, which brought him much inspiration. He promised himself that he would never go back to his previous way of living.

Three months passed since the day when he was discharged from the hospital. He spent most of that time exercising, meditating, and assisting Jane with her endeavors. Even though he had regained his strength and agility, she did not want him to leave, and he did not mind staying. Therefore, they considered making living together a permanent thing. Jane loved having him around because Jeffrey was the perfect gentleman; the fact that he was raised by his mother gave him a strong regard for women. Recently, they went to her ultrasound appointment, and it was confirmed that she was having a baby boy. They were both excited, especially Jane, who had already started planning for a boy. Jeffrey visualized the future with his unborn child, and he was sure that his whole life was about to change.

Except for some minor pain in his abdominals from time to time, he was feeling great. His strength was replenished from eating healthy and staying faithful to his exercise routine, which began at 8 a.m. every morning. Each day, he woke up around 7:30 and drove 10 minutes to the nearest recreation park, where he jogged three or four laps around the football field. Then, he would go back to the condo and used the gym in the building to do mostly calisthenic exercises. Things were going smoothly, as he dedicated his focus to establishing and building his new family. And to make it official, he used the money he had saved from working at the restaurant to buy Jane a nice diamond ring. Then, one night at the condo, while they were chilling on the balcony, he got down on one knee. And after a few words of gratitude, with the ring in his hand, he popped the question. Jane was blown away because she saw her dreams right there in front of her staring her in the eyes. Therefore, without a doubt, she gladly accepted.

"Yes!" she shouted, and her voice echoed into the universe.

Furthermore, over at the Kings' residence, Bob was spending quality time with his family. He loved every minute of it. Since he retired, he and his wife had already been on two cruises: one to Mexico and the other to the Caribbean Islands. They were planning a trip to Africa, where they will be accompanied by their children. Bob had always wanted to visit the motherland, but time never allowed since he was always working. He and Jeffrey kept in touch regularly. He would invite Jeff and his fiancé to their home for dinner every now and then. Unfortunately, the restaurant remained desolated, but Bob was in the process of receiving a settlement from the insurance company. However, they worked at their own pace, analyzing the damages, calculating numbers, and doing paperwork.

It was the first week in December of 2010, and most people were already feeling the Christmas spirit. Businesses and residences were decked with pepper lights, and the stores were filled daily with shoppers.

One Friday morning, amidst the fourth lap of his morning jog, Jeffrey was sweat-soaked, pushing himself to finish. He wanted to stop, but he kept on going, and he was able to feel the intensity throughout his body. The rhythm of his legs led his mind on another flashing journey. He pictured himself as a father as he ran, contemplating what he would do to provide for his family. He was unsure, but he was willing to do anything to push through, just like he was doing physically. He finished the lap, and then he walked back over to the parking lot where his car was parked. Before he made it back to his vehicle, he saw a colorful flyer lying on the ground, and he picked it up to check it out. It read: Primetime Promotions Presents - The Miami Apollo – Friday, December 5, 2010, at Bayfront Park in Downtown Miami. He kept the flyer, and when he sat in his car, he checked the date on his cellphone and saw that it was the 5th of December. As it came back to his memory, he was amazed that this was the same event that Cedric Williams had invited him to. He remembered that Cedric told him that he would showcase his talent at the Miami Apollo in December. Therefore, he carried the flyer home with him to show his fiancé, astonished at how surreal the timing was.

When he made it back to the condo, Jane was in the kitchen making breakfast, and he went in there and gave her a kiss. "Good morning, my love," said Jeffrey.

"Good morning, honey! How was your exercise?" she asked.

"It was great! And you won't believe what I ran into while I was out there," he replied.

"Really? What was it?" she asked with curiosity.

He handed her the flyer, but she was still clueless. Then, with a burst of excitement, he began to explain. "Do you remember me telling you months ago that Og Boe introduced me to one of his friends, who was a top player in the entertainment industry?"

She thought about it for a second, and then she replied. "Yes, I believe I do remember that. You said that he invited you to perform at one of the events."

"Exactly! I'm glad that you remember. Well, look at what I found on the ground at the park today," said Jeffrey, as he pointed at the flyer that she was holding.

She scanned it quickly with her eyes, and then, she realized what was happening. "Wait. Is this the flyer of that event?" she asked.

"Bingo!" Jeffrey replied.

"Oh my God, baby! I totally forgot about this, you know, with everything that has happened," she admitted.

"Don't feel bad," said Jeffrey. "I forgot about it myself. But yes, that is the flyer to the event, and it is actually going down tonight!"

"Unbelievable!" said Jane, smiling with excitement. "Jeff, I think you should call the guy."

"I was thinking the same thing," said Jeffrey, as he took his phone out of his pocket. They smiled as he dialed the number on the flyer.

The phone rang a couple times, and then someone answered.

"Primetime Promotions! This is Angela speaking. How may I help you?" the lady asked.

"Good morning, ma'am," Jeffrey replied. "May I please speak to Mr. Cedric Williams? Tell him that it is Jeffrey Jacob."

"Sure, hold for a minute. Let me connect you," said the lady, who was one of Mr. William's secretaries.

"No problem," Jeffrey replied. He was surprised that Cedric was even available.

After about a minute or two, a voice came on the other end of the phone. "Hello, good morning. This is Cedric."

"Good morning, Mr. Williams. This is Jeffrey, Og Boe peoples."

Cedric was excited. "Man, you kidding! Is this Kreation?" he asked.

"Yes, sir, with a K that is," said Jeffrey, and they both laughed.

"Youngblood, where have you been? You know how long I've been waiting to hear from you?" Cedric asked.

"Man, I been in the hospital in critical condition. It took me a few months to recover, but I'm up and running now," said Jeffrey.

"Oh, ok, that explains why I didn't see you at Boe's funeral," Cedric replied.

"Exactly! I was shot twice during the same incident when he died. Don't worry, I will fill you in on all the details later," said Jeffrey.

"Really? I know nothing much about what happened. I just heard that he was involved in a shootout," said Cedric. Then, he continued. "Well, I'm glad to hear that you're back on your feet. And it's funny how you called today, and the Miami Apollo is tonight. You know, the stage is yours if you want it."

"Absolutely! Man, honestly, I feel like it is primetime. Put me on the list," Jeffrey replied.

"Perfect! Say less," said Cedric. "Showtime is from 7 to 10 p.m. meet me backstage, no later than 6."

"That sounds like a plan. Thank you, Cedric! I'll see you later," Jeffrey replied.

"No pressure, youngblood, be safe," said Cedric, and then he hung up the phone.

When the line disconnected, Jane yelled. "Oh my God, baby, it's official!" Then, tears of joy began to roll from her eyes as they hugged and squeezed each other.

The breakfast was ready. She had made veggie omelets and pancakes, served with fresh fruit and orange juice. They sat together and ate, and it was a healthy breakfast. There was much joy in the air that morning because Little Jeff's moment was approaching, and he knew it. Jane had a class to attend, which started at 11 a.m., so she went and got dressed while Jeffrey took on the kitchen duties after eating. She was in the middle of her second trimester, and so far, she was able to maintain her regular schedule. In Jeffrey's eyes, she was one in a million. He decided to do some reciting while his fiancé was away at school. The only thing he could think about was the upcoming show. For him, the perfection of the timing was a sign from the universe; he visualized the experience being a success. The countdown had begun, and he was only a few hours away from his big opportunity.

Chapter 18

Jane had two classes to attend that day. When they were finished, she wasted no time getting back home. Nothing was going to make her miss her man's first significant performance. By 3 p.m., she was back home, and she and Jeffrey began to get themselves together to head out. The show was held at Bayfront Park, only 20 minutes from the condo where they lived. They decided to go out for dinner, and from there, they would head straight to the venue. Jeffrey brought out his best outfit, and Jane wore an elegant dress. They made a beautiful couple. Dinner that evening was at the Cheesecake Factory. Jeffrey ordered a Patrón margarita with his meal to compliment the way he was feeling. Time passed quickly, and around 5 p.m., they wrapped things up at the restaurant and made their way to Bayfront Park.

The traffic downtown was hectic, especially since it was the holiday season. There were many festivities and lots of people on vacation. However, they made it to the venue 30 minutes early.

"Good afternoon, my name is Jeffrey Jacob, a.k.a. Kreation. I should be on the list of performers," said Jeffrey to the guards at the gate when they arrived.

"Okay, sit tight," one of the security guards replied, while the other one made a phone call to Cedric Williams.

"Hey, boss, a guy is here with a female who says that his name is Kreation," said the guard to Cedric, who had answered immediately.

"Yes, please let them in, and give them backstage passes," Cedric replied. "Tell them that I will be waiting for them at the entrance."

Therefore, the guards did what they were told, and Jeffrey drove through the gates and parked in the designated area. He and Jane walked hand in hand, following the signs to the backstage door. The park was almost filled with people, and minute after minute, they were still coming in large groups. When Jeffrey and his fiancé made it to the backstage entrance, Mr. Williams was there waiting for them as he promised. Of course, he was busy, multitasking with about ten things at once, but he happily greeted the couple.

"Kreation in the building! What's popping, youngblood?" Cedric asked, and then they hugged and laughed.

"What's good, big homie? I'm cooling," Jeffrey replied. Then, he introduced Jane. "Meet my fiancé, Jane. Jane, this is Cedric."

"Nice to meet you. You guys are beautiful together," said Cedric, as he reached out his hand for a handshake.

"Thank you. It's nice to meet you too, Cedric," Jane replied as she shook his hand gently.

"I can't help but to notice a baby on the way," said Cedric, gesturing to her stomach.

They all laughed, and Jeffrey replied. "Yes, sir! It's official."

"Well, it's only right! Congratulations to you both," said Cedric. Then, he continued. "So, Kreation, are you ready for tonight?"

Jeffrey replied with confidence. "Man, I was born ready for tonight! I can't wait to let them feel my pain."

"That's the attitude!" Cedric exclaimed, and then he pointed down the hall. "Well, there are dressing rooms around that corner, in case you want to go there and get settled. Showtime starts in about an hour, and I still have a few things to get situated."

"No doubt. We're gonna hit up one of those dressing rooms in the meanwhile. Thanks again, man, for everything!" Jeffrey replied.

"Say less. I got you," said Cedric.

Then, he resumed his multitasking duties while Jeffrey and Jane went towards the dressing rooms. Backstage was busy, but everyone seemed excited and in a good mood; they were all friendly. The atmosphere was warm and welcoming, and Jeffrey felt like it was where he belonged, right there amongst the entertainers.

The Miami Apollo is a nationwide competition held annually. People from all around the world would travel to Miami to attend the show. Cedric Williams is the chairman and the overseer who cultivated the idea a few years ago. Since then, it has grown tremendously, and 2010 was the show's 5th anniversary. The purpose of the competition was to find new talent and give that individual or group a jumpstart towards stardom. The event was sponsored by several major record labels and publishers of different genres. This year the winner would win 50 thousand dollars, a trip to London, and one year of access to whichever company they needed to further their career. The second-place winner will receive 25 thousand dollars and six months of access to their desired company. Third place winner will only receive 10 thousand dollars; however, each performer would get much recognition because the show would be televised. In addition, to keep things interesting, there were usually two or three guest celebrities, who performed before and after the amateurs took the stage. This year, Ciara was going to open to get the audience up on their feet. Then, Chance the Rapper would be closing out after the performances.

The couple found an empty dressing room, and they went in there to relax until it was showtime. It was the biggest night of Jeffrey's life, and he wanted to use it for all that it was worth. He was going to do it for everything he had been through over the past years and for everyone he lost to gun violence. However, his biggest motivation was his unborn child because he was determined to secure a brighter future for his son.

The show started, and the host was on stage, getting the crowd hyped as he introduced Ciara for the opening performance. Jeffrey and

Jane drew close to the stage to get a good view. They were up close and personal with the entertainers as they enjoyed their backstage experience. By that time, the park was filled with thousands of people from around the world to witness history in the making. The event was sold-out, which was a normal thing for most of Primetime Promotion's events.

Furthermore, Ciara took the stage, and she started doing what she did best, singing and dancing while the crowd went wild. Her energy was top-level as the rhythm from the live band sank deep into the people's souls. Jeffrey paid full attention, and Jane was also tuned in, so much that the performance gave her the chills. Then, after Ciara got the crowd on their feet, the amateur performances began. Young Jeffrey was prudent, patiently waiting for his moment, feeling slightly nervous but far from timid. The competition was on, as different artists took the stage to showcase their talent. About an hour and a half into the show, Cedric came looking for Jeffrey.

"Hey, Kreation, are you ready?" Cedric asked.

"Yes, sir, like I never been," said Jeffrey.

"That's good because you're up next," Cedric replied.

"Cool! Let's do it," said Jeffrey with enthusiasm.

The only word on Little Jeff's mind at that time was SHOWTIME! The artist who was on stage closed out his performance, and the audience applauded.

Then, the host proceeded through the curtains and began: "Miami! Give it up one more time for Taz, from Grind Hard Music! That was a spectacular performance." The audience cheered, and the host continued. "Now, this next artist that I'm about to call to the stage is a poet who is coming to you live from the trenches, from the wards of New Orleans to the streets of Miami. He lost both of his parents to gun violence, and now he is filled with pain and passion. Without further adieu, please help me to welcome our young brother, Kreation!"

The introduction grabbed everyone's attention, and the audience was now anxious as they applauded. As Jeffrey walked, he remembered the dream he had when he was 12 years old – the dream when he was running away from something and then was lifted and carried to the glamorous city to perform in front of thousands of people. For a moment, everyone was quiet, and then Jeffrey closed his eyes and thought about God's unconditional love. Jeffrey's broken heart mended as he approached the microphone stand. He then realized that he was living his dream, and therefore, he was ready to pick up from where it was cut off. He grabbed the microphone and began to survey the crowd. Penetrated by the stare of the many faces, he began to improvise.

"The Power of Love!
Why do you give it when I do not deserve it?
When my actions are worthy, then I expect it.
Why is it still effective when I compromise?
Is it so genuine that it still abides?
Indeed, it is the strongest force!
That unconditional love from above,
It is the only remedy for a dying soul.
Please, Lord, guide me through these phases,
And I promise that I will forever stand for your love!"

Everyone was silent as he poured his heart out into every line, and when he was done, tears began to flow from his eyes. The audience broke its silence and started screaming and shouting, applauding as Kreation waved and walked off the stage. Even though it was short, he got his message across, and the sincerity was felt. Cedric and his fiancé were there waiting, with big smiles on their faces, when he made it back behind the curtains.

"Way to go, youngblood!" said Cedric, as he gave him a high five.

"Man, thank you for the opportunity! This is great," Jeffrey replied.

Then, he and Jane hugged and kissed. She was impressed with his performance and turned on by his confidence. The show went on, and a few more artists took the stage, each of them coming with their A-games. After the first round of performances, the host announced the finalists. There were only six finalists from a total of 18 contestants, and fortunately, Kreation was one of them. They all had to do one more selection, from which three would be eliminated, and three winners would be chosen. Jeffrey got over his nervousness and was comfortable going into the second round. He was planning on having fun with his next selection. When he came to bless the stage once again, he went with one of his favorite poems – "So, I Write." It was another intense performance, and when he finished, everyone stood in ovation. Placed in the scrolls of history, that night was one to remember.

Chapter 19

Three years later. The lovebirds stared each other in the eyes as Jane tried hard to hold her tears back.

The pastor announced. "With all the blessings of the Lord, I now pronounce you, husband and wife. You may kiss the bride!"

Jeffrey gently placed his hands around her waist, and she held his neck as they enjoyed a wet kiss. Everyone applauded, and some even cried because it was amazing to see a young couple who were truly in love.

The pastor went on. "Ladies and gentlemen, let me be the first to introduce to you, Mr. and Mrs. Jacob!"

Everyone cheered as Jeffrey looked away into the audience and waved at their son, Jeffrey Junior, who was sitting with Jane's parents. It was an unforgettable moment as the newlyweds walked back down the aisle hand in hand. The feeling was tremendous, and it was time to celebrate. Most of the people at the wedding were there on Jane's behalf, her family and friends from school. To represent Jeffrey, Bob, his family, and Cedric Williams and his beautiful wife were there. Cedric was looking sharp in his black and white tailor-made tuxedo and his Kangol hat. All the bride's planning that went into the ceremony and the reception turned out to be successful. The venue was filled with family and friends, and the energy in the building was electrifying to the end. During the reception, everyone danced and fellowshipped.

Jeffrey and Cedric Williams had kept in touch regularly since the

Miami Apollo three years before. Since that night, Kreation, as he was better known, was made into a household name. Even though he won second place in the competition, his life changed dramatically. In many aspects, he was still triumphant. From facing his fears and overcoming his struggles, poverty and the street life, were now things of the distant past.

That night at the Apollo, first-place was given to a teenage girl, whose voice gave you goosebumps whenever she sang. Her name was Destiny, and she was in town from Chicago. The selection that she performed in the final round shook the foundations, and she took the prize. Therefore, Kreation did not go to London, but he won 25 thousand dollars and a recording contract for his spoken word. He was grateful and content, and because Destiny was from out of town, the fans cherished him as their hometown superstar. Knowing Cedric Williams was better than knowing a thousand people because he had connections to almost anything you could imagine. He proved to be a good friend and a reliable source, and come to find out, one of his many business ventures was real estate investing. He educated Jeffrey on the process of owning property and even located a startup investment, which was a duplex in Liberty City that was on the market for $60,000. The units were two-bedroom, one-bath units, and the tenants paid $900 monthly per unit. Jeffrey was given access to a wonderful opportunity. Therefore, he made the duplex his first rental property with a 15 percent down payment plus closing costs.

He also earned a contract with Atlantic Records and was given six months to utilize the company to his advantage. He produced an album of him reciting a collection of poems with live instruments playing softly in the background. The album contained 23 poems, in which he poured out his heart with unique style, resulting in nothing less than a masterpiece. The production went viral, and then he nailed a few more notable performances; Kreation the Poet was a trending topic.

A year after the wedding, one early morning, Jeffrey received a call from Ziona.

"Hey, Jeffrey. I have some bad news. Bob did not wake up this morning. He died in his sleep," said Ziona, and then she started crying.

"Aw, man, I'm so sorry to hear that," Jeffrey replied sadly, and as he thought about it, tears began to roll down from his eyes as well. The news was tragic, and Jeffrey felt like he lost a part of himself because Bob was his mentor and his source of guidance.

No one saw it coming because he was still strong and healthy even though the elder was 85 years old. It was heartbreaking, but the only thing promised to a man in this life is death. Bobby King was a man who lived his creed, one who reached his goals and made his dreams a reality. About a year after the restaurant's massacre, he came to terms with the insurance company for a settlement of half a million dollars, which was the supplement for a total loss of his business. Then, two years ago, he and his family went on the pilgrimage of a lifetime to different countries of the motherland. They were away for three months and visited countries like Egypt, Ethiopia, Ghana, and Nigeria. Since Bob retired, that trip was on the top of his to-do list, and fortunately, he was able to check it off before he left the earth. He was the ideal role model, a cornerstone of the community who will always remain in the hearts of many people, especially his family, including Jeffrey. Funeral arrangements were made to suit a large capacity. The service was scheduled for two weeks later to give the many friends and relatives time to fly in from overseas.

Two weeks later. The turnout of Bobby King's funeral was like the Martin Luther King parade in Miami. People from everywhere flooded the streets, and most of them were locals from Opa Locka, showing their respect for the late icon. It was a sad occasion as the family mourned their loss. Still, during the ceremony, the preacher encouraged everyone to be happy because Bob was in a better place. His loved ones were profoundly grateful to see the reflection of the old man's impact on so many people, and they were inspired to carry on the legacy.

A month after the funeral, Ziona called Jeffrey. "Hey Jeff, come on over to the house as soon as possible. I have something to show you," said Ziona with a tone of urgency.

"Okay, Ms. Ziona. I'm on my way right now," Jeffrey replied, and then he wasted no time getting there.

When he made it to the Kings' house, Ziona showed him Bob's will. He was surprised to see that his name was mentioned in it. The old man had divided the ownership of the business into quarters. He left it with his wife, his two children, and Jeffrey, noting that Jeffrey Jacob was the man with the drive to resurrect the business. Little Jeff was honored, and immediately, he began to brainstorm the idea of bringing Bobby's Meals back to life in the community. Even though it was almost five years since the restaurant had been out of commission, people were still talking about how good the food tasted. The family agreed that with dedication, the right team, and the right plan, the restaurant could be back at the level where it was performing before the shooting, maybe even better. However, time was of the essence, so Jeffrey arranged a meeting with Ziona, Jahfari, and Makyah, to organize a business plan. They were planning on making the restaurant a franchise, a plan that would benefit their grandchildren's children if it were correctly maintained. The team decided to launch a restaurant in a more popular location. Then after about a year, they would reopen another one in Opa Locka. They knew that the plan would work since the restaurant's legacy was already well known, and plus, Bob left a hefty budget for them to work with. Ziona, who was 79 years old, made it clear that she wanted no part in running the business except for releasing the finances needed for the investment and teaching the recipes for the meals and the natural juices.

With the help of Cedric Williams and his real estate ties, they found the perfect spot for the restaurant, right in the heart of South Beach Miami, off 16th street and Washington Avenue. Jahfari was a licensed contractor, so he got his crew together, and they went to work on the building right away. After the labor and inspection process, the restaurant was ready to open its doors to the public in just a few months.

Bobby's Meals on South Beach! It was a brilliant idea, and the grand opening was like a homecoming celebration. Many people from the inner city were there to witness it. Jeffrey was a proud part-owner and the business manager. He hired two cooks and a waitress, making sure that everyone was professionally trained.

It was early June of 2015. Jeffrey Jacob was now 26 years old, and his son, Junior, was four. His family was financially stable, managing their responsibilities, and everyone was happy. Jane completed her studies and earned her master's degree, and after she graduated, they celebrated for about a week straight. She was working in her dream career as a full-time banker, and she was loving every minute of it. The income that she and Jeffrey were generating and the money they were saving together made it possible for Junior to be a millionaire by the time he reached 18. Jeffrey was grateful to see how well his life turned out, and he often reflected on the many times when he escaped death itself on his journey to the mountain top.

One Friday afternoon, he pulled his 2015 BMW 5 series up to Junior's babysitter's house. Her name is Ms. Shannon, and she was a lady who Jane knew since she and her brother were growing up. Jeffrey was there to pick up Junior, so he went up to the door and rang the doorbell.

"Well, good afternoon, Mr. Jacob," said Ms. Shannon when she answered the door.

"Hello, Ms. Shannon, good afternoon. Is Junior ready?" Jeffrey asked.

"As a matter of fact, he is," she replied. Then, she tilted her head back and yelled: "Junior, your dad is here!"

Seconds later, Junior came running to the door with his backpack in his hand, and then he yelled with excitement when he saw his father. "Daddy!"

"What's up, my big boy? Are you ready?" Jeffrey asked as he stooped down to hug his son.

"Yes, sir!" Junior replied.

They waved goodbye to the babysitter, and then they walked towards the vehicle. "See you later, Ms. Shannon," said Junior.

"Later, guys, drive safe," she replied.

"Hop in the front seat," said Jeffrey.

Junior, who had been reaching for the back door, got in the front gladly and buckled up. Jeffrey buckled his seatbelt, and then they drove off.

"So, how was your day, son?"

"It was good, dad. I was drawing in my art book."

"That sounds like a lot of fun," said Jeffrey.

He was still getting used to being a father. However, with a two-parent household, everything was going smoothly. Jane was at the condo preparing dinner while Jeffrey and their son laughed and talked on their way to her.

After a while, Junior asked. "Hey, Dad, can you tell me the story about what happened when I was in mommy's stomach?"

Jeffrey smiled. He had told Junior a long time ago that many bad things happened when his mother was pregnant with him and that he would tell him all about it when he gets old enough to understand. Junior did not forget, and he felt like he was ready to hear the story. However, Jeffrey knew that the time was not right for specific details, so he summed it up the best way possible.

"Son, if it was not for God Almighty, your dad would not be alive right now." Jeffrey began, and then he looked over at Junior and saw himself as a child. His son was listening carefully, and so, he went on. "You should always strive to be the best that you can be. Like a wise man once told me: 'In all that you do, you must remain conscious of the consciousness that is within you.' You understand?"

Junior nodded as the wise words echoed in his head. "Yes, Dad, I got it!"

"Ok, Son, I love you," said Jeffrey.

"I love you too, Daddy!" Junior replied.

They were almost home, and Jeffrey felt a tingle in his stomach; he thought his wife should be about done with dinner. So, he stepped on the gas, and the BMW blended into the ongoing traffic.